Revenge Served HOT

A CRIME ANTHOLOGY

Suzan Harden

This is a work of fiction. All characters, organizations and events in this anthology are products of the author's imagination and are not to be construed as real. Any resemblance to persons, living or dead, is entirely coincidental.

REVENGE SERVED HOT
ISBN - 978-1-64918-011-7

Published by Angry Sheep Publishing
Findlay, Ohio

Interior Design by JW Manus
Cover Design by Suzan Harden

More by Suzan Harden

Bloodlines
Blood Magick
Zombie Love
Zombie Confidential
Zombie Wedding
Amish, Vamps & Thieves
Blood Sacrifice
Love, War & a Bulldog
Zombie Goddess
Ravaged
Sacrificed
Reality Bites
Ghouls in the Grocery Store
Resurrected
Bloodlines Shorts Anthology
Bloodlines: The First Boxed Set

Seasons of Magick
Spring
Summer
Autumn
Winter
The Seasons of Magick Anthology

Justice
Sword and Sorceress 28
("Justice")
Sword and Sorceress 30
("Diplomacy in the Dark")
Justice: The Beginning
A Question of Balance
A Modicum of Truth
A Matter of Death
A Touch of Mother
A Twist of Love
A Virtue of Child
A Hand of Father
A Measure of Knowledge
(Coming Soon)

The Justice Thalia Stories
Snowfall
Murder Most Fowl
The Sweetest Poison

888-555-HERO
Hero De Facto
Hero Ad Hoc
Hero De Novo
A Very Hero Christmas
Hero De Jure
Hero In Camera
Hero Amicus Curiae
A Very Hero Wedding
Hero Ad Litem
(Coming Soon)

Solar System Services, Inc.
Alone Is Not Lonely

Millersburg Magick Mysteries
Spells and Sleuths
Fae and Felonies
Magick and Murder

Soccer Moms of the Apocalypse
Pestilence in Pumpkin Spice
(Coming Soon)
Famine In French Vanilla
War in White Chocolate
Death in Double Mocha

Miscellaneous
Sword and Sorceress 31
("Pig-Headed")
Sword and Sorceress 32
("Unexpected")
Practical Witches
Revenge Served Hot

For updates, news, and giveaways, join Suzan's mailing list or visit her website at www.suzanharden.com. You can also check her out on Twitter or Facebook.

Contents

Dance with the Devil

It should have been an easy job. In. Out. No faffing about as my foster mom used to say. Charlee told me not to accept it. Said she didn't have a good feeling about it. I should have listened to my wife.

As confidential specialists, we throw clients off when we first meet. Charlee's the muscle, even though I'm a foot taller than her. No one takes a petite blonde as a serious threat until it's too late. I'm the brains of the team.

Most of the time.

Honestly, the reason I accepted the job was the opportunity to go to Vegas. I love that city. I could make a decent living playing black jack. The real trick is not to get greedy when counting cards. That's where most people screw up.

I keep trying to talk Charlee into moving there permanently. She says she hates the sweating and the fake people. In reality, I think her reluctance was because she's never stayed in one place longer than she needed to, so I was on the losing end of that argument. Her foster parents weren't good people.

However, nothing would make me give up Charlee. Not even Las Vegas

We entered a diner off the beaten path to meet our client, one of those places where the red vinyl seats and Formica and aluminum tables are held together by a layer of grease. The dim lighting was maybe a couple of watts brighter than a strip club's. One-armed bandits jangled, buzzed, and made an annoying ton of racket, just like in nearly every other establishment in the state of Nevada. You couldn't escape the noise. On the plus side, the sweet siren call of tobacco filled the joint despite the recent changes to the laws about not smoking in any public places. Damn, I missed cigarettes, but I'd given 'em up for Charlee. Her asthma couldn't handle the smoke.

The waitress gave us the once over when I asked for a booth, but she didn't say a word. You'd think in the twenty-first century people would get over seeing a black man with a white woman. Charlee insisted it was the fact she looked under age with no makeup and wearing jeans and a t-shirt. I went along with her view though I knew better.

We said someone would be joining us and ordered soft drinks. The waitress made a face and stomped off, obviously thinking she wasn't getting much of a tip from us. Self-fulfilling prophesy there.

I picked out our client as soon as she entered the diner. Elderly white woman. Lines and creases on face and hands. Gray hair teased high to disguise the thinning spots. Pink cardigan and white blouse with black polyester slacks. Orthotic shoes. An oversized blue paisley purse by Vera Bradley was the most expensive thing on her other than her wedding ring. She should have been at the bingo hall, not meeting us in a seedy, off-the-Strip, greasy spoon. She spotted us and walked toward the booth with the careful steps of someone worried about falling.

We only took clients through referrals. My buddy Taejoon had a knack for picking the right folks, which was the reason I pitched to Charlee for taking the job. She had merely smiled at me and shook her head. I never could fool her, but still, how could we turn down an elderly widow who needed us?

The Vegas thing was just a bonus. Right?

I rose like a gentleman and held out my hand. "Mrs. Whitcomb?"

"A pleasure to meet you, Mr. Hodges." She took my hand and shook it, her grip remarkably firm for someone her age. She nodded to my wife. "Mrs. Hodges."

Charlee didn't correct the client. She hated being called Mrs. Hodges even though we'd been married fifteen years. That should have been my second clue.

I gestured at the bench I'd just vacated. "Have a seat. Our mutual friend said someone stole something from you."

She slid into the booth, talking before I even had a chance to sit next to Charlee. "It's my grandson Derrick." Mrs. Lily Whitcomb pulled a tissue from her left sweater sleeve and dabbed at her eyes. "He took my husband's ashes. I want you to get them back for me."

"Your husband's ashes?" I tried to keep my face as bland as possible despite the icky feeling running along my skin. "Why would Derrick steal his grandfather's ashes?"

"Walter wasn't Derrick's grandfather. He was my third husband." She sniffed and swiped at her nose with her tissue before she pulled out an envelope. The contents she removed were a photo of Derrick and one of Walter, both white men, plus a slip of paper with Derrick's home address and phone number. From the thickness of the envelope, half our recovery fee was inside, too.

"It would help if we had Derrick's work address and number, too." I opened my leather folder and removed my pen.

"There isn't one." Mrs. Whitcomb replaced the contents and shoved the envelope to me across the table. "He works from his house. He's a writer." She shook her head. "He was always such a flighty boy."

"Why?" Charlee said. Her bluntness puts off a lot of people. On the other hand, it can cut through a lot of bullshit.

"Why what, dear?" Mrs. Whitcomb gave her a tremulous smile.

"Why would Derrick take the ashes?" Charlee cocked her head. "And how do you know it was him?"

"I have a teddy bear with a nanny cam in it sitting in

my living room. My granddaughter Gail set it up for me when my things started to go missing a month ago. Right after Walter's death." Mrs. Whitcomb reached into her ugly paisley purse and pulled out a flash drive. "Here's a copy of the video showing Derrick take Walter's ashes." She sighed and held out the black plastic device to me. "As for why he took them, I have no idea. He and Walter had been friendly, but not overly close. And I thought Derrick held me in the same affection that I held him. All I can tell you is I want my Walter back."

"Have you confronted Derrick about taking the ashes?" I asked as I took the flash drive from her. "And does anyone else in the family know about the theft?"

Mrs. Whitcomb shook her head. "No, I haven't confronted him. I didn't know what to say to him. And I didn't want the rest of the family to think less of Derrick. Gail only knows because I needed her assistance to transfer the video from my computer to the flash drive. She promised not to tell anyone and to let me resolve this my way."

"You said other things had gone missing," Charlee said. "What things?"

"Nothing truly valuable. Odd things. Like a silver frame. Walter's old video camera. My hair brush."

"Your hairbrush?" I asked. I didn't have to look at Charlee. The other two items could be easily pawned. "What type of hairbrush?"

"A plastic white one from Walmart." Mrs. Whitcomb

looked equally perplexed. "It has the rubber grip." She held up her hands. "My arthritis makes it hard to hold any other kind of brush."

Okay, it wasn't my imagination. Taking the hairbrush made no damn sense.

I watched the video and double-checked the information Mrs. Whitcomb had given us concerning Derrick on my laptop while Charlee drove. "It would be stupid for him to keep the urn at his house," I muttered.

"Are you finding a storage unit in his name? An apartment? Anything?"

"No." I slammed down my laptop lid. "Break in and search his place while he's picking up groceries?"

"It would take too much time, and I know how bad you want to hit the blackjack tables." She shot me a sly smile before she returned her attention to the street.

"Not the FBI gambit again." I groaned. "It's too damn hot outside to wear suits."

"You should have thought of that before accepting a job in the desert." She sounded far too happy about this. "Make a copy of the video."

"Blackmail isn't your usual style," I teased.

"Not blackmail. Proof of theft. Mrs. Whitcomb will forgo charges for the return of the urn."

If that was the story Charlee wanted to spin, fine. I hoped Derrick cooperated because impersonating the

FBI would tip him off Mrs. Whitcomb knew he'd taken Walter's ashes.

Derrick sagged in his doorway when Charlee and I displayed our fake FBI IDs. The kid was barely taller than her, with dirty blond hair and sharp pointed features. He wore a black and yellow t-shirt with the logo of a popular superhero. His clean jeans bore the strategic rips that were popular a generation ago.

He gestured for us to enter his house. Charlee sat on the living room couch with Derrick and laid out her planned speech while I stood and glared at the kid.

"I don't have the ashes I took from Grandma's place," Derrick said.

"Where are they?" Charlee asked.

"With a friend at the UNLV Medical School. He's testing the remains." He clutched his knees so tight the skin over his knucklebones turned white.

"Testing the remains for what?" Charlee prompted.

Derrick sighed before he called out, "Walter? You might as well come out. It's the FBI."

A grunt and shuffling noises came from the back of the house. Charlee stood and drew her gun from her waist holster. An elderly man in blue and white striped pajamas shambled into the living room with his walker. His mug matched the photo Mrs. Whitcomb had given us of her late third husband.

"Don't arrest the boy. Derrick's only guilty of helping me try to prove who wants to kill me." Walter's garrulous voice carried a brittle edge.

"Murder you?" I stared at the elderly man. "We thought you were already dead."

"Not for lack of trying on my beloved wife's part," he snapped.

"Why are you having the ashes in the urn tested?" Charlee looked as confused as I felt.

"Because we think they're really my biological grandfather's ashes." Derrick blew out a deep breath. "And we think my grandmother's a black widow."

<hr>

For the next hour, Derrick and Walter laid out their case. Gerald, Mrs. Whitcomb's first husband and Derrick's biological grandfather, disappeared when Derrick's father was a teenager. The sheriff's department presumed Gerald had drowned when his boat was found drifting on Lake Tahoe.

It wasn't like they could drag Tahoe for the body. It was too damn deep.

The second husband Bart had drowned in the pool at the house in Reno where he and Mrs. Whitcomb had lived at the time. According to the coroner's report, Bart had been drunk and presumed to have fallen in while Mrs. Whitcomb traveled to Palm Springs with some girlfriends.

"Sounds normal, right?" Walter made a derisive sound. "Lily had some bad luck with her men. That's what I thought when I met her a year later."

"She told us that you and Derrick weren't close," Charlee said.

Derrick and Walter looked at each other.

"I ain't embarrassed, but you sure you want to tell them?" One of Walter's bushy eyebrows rose.

Once again, Derrick blew out his breath. "I love Barry Manilow."

I don't know what I was expecting, but that wasn't it. "And?"

"C'mon. A guy my age enjoying Manilow's music?" Pink flushed up Derrick's face. "Walter found my secret stash of CDs."

"You still have CDs?" Charlee's incredulous expression would have been funny if we weren't talking attempted murder.

"I used to play with Barry's band back in the day in New York," Walter said. "I offered to set up a meeting for the kid. Lily was heading out of town with some friends to New Orleans. It would be mine and the kid's secret. I knew the family would tease the shit out of him. He gets enough crap from them for being a writer."

Walter shook his head. "I'd been gradually feeling crappy over the first three days she was gone. I take nitro-glycerin for angina. It didn't seem to be doing anything. Derrick found me on the kitchen floor the morning we were supposed to go see Barry."

"He refused to go to a hospital." Derrick shot his step-grandfather a dirty look.

"Didn't trust those buggers," Walter grumbled.

"Let me guess." Charlee smirked. "Derrick's buddy at the medical school said you overdosed on nitro even though you were taking the prescribed amount."

Walter's jaw dropped.

Derrick swallowed hard. "The acetaminophen Walter takes for his arthritis. The contents of the capsules were laced with nitro. H-how did you know?"

"It's how I'd get rid of my husband," she said.

We'd have to discuss Charlee's plan to murder me later. For now, I ignored it. "Why didn't you two go to the local police once you knew the pills had been switched?" I asked.

"Because Grandma called me, saying Walter had been found dead up in the mountains. She said he'd been filming wildlife and must have slipped and fallen into a ravine." Derrick's greenish cast was understandable. Regular people were unaccustomed to the vulgarities of the human race. "Predators had gotten to the corpse. She said that's why she had the body cremated."

"And you took the video camera from her house, looking for proof," I said. "I don't get the silver picture frame or the hair brush though."

Derrick looked on the verge of tears. "The frame held a lock of Grandpa Gerald's hair."

"And you don't think your grandmother's real name is Lily Whitcomb," I finished.

The kid's shoulders started to shake. Walter put a comforting arm around his step-grandson.

⁓

At a strip mall, Charlee and I sat in our non-descript SUV with the A/C turned up high. Something told me the kid wasn't making this shit up, even if he was a writer. No one would ever believe something this bizarre.

I stated the obvious. "We can't fulfill the contract."

"No shit," Charlee grumbled. "What I don't get is how she tossed the body into the ravine. She could barely stay upright."

"Or where she stashed him for the last twenty years?" I quipped. "Does it really matter at this point?"

"She's not a good person," Charlee growled.

"We aren't either if we go back on our word about a client's privacy."

"I am not refunding her fee. She lied to us." Charlee glared at me.

"I didn't say we would," I protested.

"And what about our rules?" she snapped.

We'd both had pretty shitty childhoods with serious juvenile records. Ironically, it meant we tried to help peo-ple in trouble even if our methods weren't exactly legal.

But we sure as hell weren't going to give Lily Whitcomb

another opportunity to murder Walter. Or dispose of Derrick as her only loose end.

"We will have to break one of them." I turned to look at Charlee.

"Not that one." She stared at me like I suggested we go totally straight.

"Yes, that one."

She leaned back against the headrest and groaned. "I swear to God, honey, if we get arrested, I will kill you."

"I thought you loved prison," I teased.

"The only reason I stayed in that French prison for a month was their delicious breakfast soufflés. And this ain't France."

———

At least, I could honestly tell Mrs. Whitcomb neither the urn nor the ashes were at Derrick's house. I also told her we had a plan for retrieval, but it would take another couple of days.

As I suspected, Tae-joon had a homicide detective who owed him a favor. It didn't take much to prove motive. Not when each successive husband was richer than the last.

Derrick's boyfriend was the mysterious medical student at UNLV. He promptly turned everything over to Tae-joon's detective friend. As poor Derrick suspected, the guy in the urn was his missing biological grandfather. Mrs. Whitcomb's arrest made the headlines.

Or I should say Judy Nesmith's arrest. The detective found the storage unit with the freezer in Carson City under Walter's name. There was enough evidence inside the freezer to show Gerald had been there. The odd thing was the proprietor said it wasn't a woman, but a man who'd rented the unit. After twenty-five years, he couldn't pick out the man in question from the pictures he was shown, but he did recognize Judy as having been at the facility the previous month with a younger man who resembled Derrick.

Except Derrick had an alibi. He and Walter had gone to meet Barry Manilow after all.

The police couldn't find the accomplice, and Judy refused to spill the beans about him. For a frail physique, she had an iron will.

Once the cops had finished their investigation, and Judy was denied bail, Walter moved back into his house and invited us to his so-called resurrection celebration. In Walter's study, the four of us were toasting to his new life.

"I can't believe she kept Grandpa's body for the last twenty-five years," Derrick said as he shuddered.

Walter grunted. "Probably forgot about it until she needed it."

I lifted my glass of expensive red wine. "We're just glad the matter is finished."

"It's not finished," a feminine voice said. "Tell them the rest."

We all pivoted to find a young woman with sharp

features and dirty blond hair standing in the doorway of the study. If she stuck her medium length hair under a cap and didn't wear makeup, she could almost pass for Derrick. With shaking hands, she held a gun.

"G-gail?" Derrick stammered.

"Tell Walter the truth," she snarled at me. "That you aren't FBI. That Grandmother hired you to retrieve those damn ashes."

Derrick and Walter both stared at Charlee and me.

"Of course." Charlee smacked her head. "You were supposed to make sure Walter was dead. When he disappeared, Judy needed someone to help her get Gerald's body and Walter's car up to the mountains."

"Why, Gail?" Derrick stared at his cousin. "She killed our own grandfather."

"Pfft." Gail raised her chin. "It's not like we ever knew him."

"Let me guess," I said, taking a step away from the others. "Judy promised to leave everything to you."

Gail snorted. "Like I believed her. I knew she was planning to take off with the money as soon as her lawyer got everything transferred to her name. I planned to get rid of her as soon as that was finished. But then my dumbass cousin decided to get in the middle of this."

"Shooting four people is a little harder to hide," I said. If I kept her attention on me, Charlee could take out Gail.

"Home invasions happen all the time." Gail flashed

a vicious grin. "Just more of our family's bad luck." Her finger tightened on the trigger, the barrel aimed at me.

Charlee rushed her, shoving Gail's arm up. No one realizes how damn loud a gun is, but the fact I heard it meant I was okay.

The gun fired again as the women wrestled. Charlee stiffened and slowly collapsed to the floor. Gail stared at my wife. All I saw was the blood.

I grabbed the heavy wine bottle from the buffet and swung it at Gail's head with all my strength. The bitch dropped like a sack of rocks.

Derrick grabbed the gun, and shaking as much as his cousin had been, he aimed it at me. "What was Gail talking about?"

As much as I wanted to rush to Charlee, I held up my hands. "Judy hired us to get the urn and ashes back from you."

"So you were impersonating the FBI?"

"Yes." I glanced at Charlee. Thank god, her chest was rising and falling. "You can call the police, but please let me help my partner."

"Put the gun down, Derrick." Walter pressed his step-grandson's hands so the barrel was no longer aimed at my head. I rushed over to my wife, ripped off my suit jacket and held it against the bullet wound in Charlee's shoulder.

"Knowing Lily, er, Judy, she didn't pay you your full fee, did she?" Walter had an amused grin on his face.

"We didn't deliver the urn and ashes to her."

"I'll pay you the rest of the fee plus a reasonable commission for saving us from Gail," he said. "But you and your lady friend need to skedaddle before the police get here."

A doctor friend of Tae-joon's stitched up Charlee without asking any questions. I got her up to our room at the Bellagio without too much fuss and tucked her into the king-sized bed.

"And you wonder why I don't want to live in Vegas." Charlee looked up at me with the slightly dazed expression from enjoying a good painkiller. "Do you think Walter would send someone to kill us?"

"What?" I sat next to her on the bed. "Why on earth would he do that?"

"In case, we figure out he was Lily/Judy's original accomplice in killing Gerald."

"That's ridiculous," I muttered. So why did icy fingers crawl up my spine?

"Then how did Gerald's body get stashed in a storage unit under Walter's name twenty-four years before he supposedly met Lily?"

"That's the drugs talking. Get some rest, baby." I leaned over and kissed Charlee's forehead. Soon, soft snores filled our suite.

I walked over and stared at the glaring neon of the

Strip. As much as I hated to admit it, Charlee was right. I should have seen it first.

We couldn't come back to Las Vegas. Not until Walter Whitcomb was dead.

Chumming the Water

"It's not illegal if you don't get caught." My criminal law professor's words still rang in my head fifteen years later.

I doubted this was what Professor Chu meant as my sister and I loaded my brother-in-law's body into the gigantic green wheelbarrow her gardener used around their Corpus Christi beach house. The fresh mix of salt and fish scent from the Gulf of Mexico made what we were doing seem so innocent.

The only lights nearby, besides those of the beach house, were a ship a couple of miles out on the water and chugging away from us. Probably a cargo ship that had departed from the port. Kristi wanted a flashlight, but I didn't want anyone who might be in one of the other beach houses or passing by on the sand to see anything. The floodlights from the deck had given us more than enough illumination to wrap the corpse in a blue plastic tarp and secure it with gardening twine.

Kristi had called me in a total panic three hours earlier.

The one smart thing she'd done when she confronted Paul was to do it in their garden rather than inside the house or on the deck. I didn't know if she meant to shoot him because of the crimes he committed or to protect herself from being named an accomplice.

It didn't matter though. Everything was working to my advantage.

No one had heard my sister double-tap her husband. Otherwise, the police would have beat me to the beach house.

We rolled the wheelbarrow down the dock and dragged the tarp-wrapped body onto Paul's expensive speedboat.

The only sounds besides our gasps and pants were the slosh-hiss of the waves and the occasional cry of a sea bird. I ordered Kristi to wash out the wheelbarrow, first in the Gulf and then dip it in her pool. The chlorine would destroy any body liquids that may have seeped from the tarp.

I never understood why anyone would install a swimming pool, much less a series of decorative ponds, with the Gulf of Mexico so close. But hell, I'd take every advantage I had.

While she cleaned out the wheelbarrow, I collected everything I would need—Kristi's Glock she used to shoot her husband, matches, and one of Paul's very sharp kitchen knives. I paused when I spotted the opened large padded envelope on the counter, the same one I'd mailed anonymously. A quick check of Paul's office confirmed the hot pink flash drive was plugged into his desktop computer. Some keystrokes verified neither Kristi nor Paul had erased the video on the tiny drive.

I pulled off the plastic keyboard guard. No sense in confirming I was in my brother-in-law's office tonight.

I shoved the keyboard guard into the reusable canvas shopping bag I'd found along with my other supplies and placed them on the speedboat. Next step, I found a net and used it to scoop out the decorative fish from the garden into a bucket. Once Kristi returned the wheelbarrow to the gardening shed, she and I carried the bucket full of gasping, flopping koi to the speedboat.

We went to the boat house for the last things I needed—my sea-worthy two-person kayak, its paddles and an extra can of gasoline. Part of me was glad Kristi and Paul didn't question why I wanted to store the kayak here. They had bought my story I needed a place to keep it while I looked for a house of my own in Houston now I was back in the States.

Once everything was secured, I told Kristi to sit down. Her initial panic had given way to numbness. Her emotional state meant she only did what I told her to do. She wasn't thinking beyond her own guilt. I untied the lines and climbed on board the speedboat.

I pressed the ignition, and Paul's speedboat purred to life. Once we were clear of the shallows, I gunned the engine, and we sped into the dark gulf. I needed deeper water before I started chumming.

Once we were far enough we couldn't see the shore, I cut the power. Kristi didn't move. She just stared at the body wrapped in blue poly tarp. I grabbed the bucket, cut up the dead fish, and tossed the bits into the Gulf waters. The koi in Paul's stupidly expensive Japanese-style garden were good for something after all.

It didn't take long for the splashing to start around the boat.

"Help me," I ordered.

Kristi rose from her seat. Together, we lifted the corpse to the gunwale. I cut the twine, and we rolled my late brother-in-law into the water.

More splashing. Louder. The boat rocked with the motion of the predators consuming the evidence.

"How could I let this happen?" Kristi wailed. She fell back into the rear passenger seat and sobbed.

"I've been wondering the same thing myself," I muttered.

She was an inky shape against the stars, but her sobs abruptly stopped, and her silence spoke volumes.

I asked anyway. "Why would anyone let her husband rape her daughter? Repeatedly?"

"I didn't know!"

Who was she trying to convince? Me or herself? She wasn't even aware how I knew. How I'd found out. She hadn't told me.

However, her denial meant she'd seen the contents of the flash drive. The one with the video of Paul raping

Maddy. The one showing Kristi in the doorway of my niece's bedroom, watching everything.

Kristi had called me after she'd killed Paul. However, she hadn't been smart enough to dispose of the other evidence.

"No." The Gulf breeze carried away my sigh. "You enjoyed watching the show."

"You don't understand." She stood and reached into the bag. Looking for the gun. So I was expendable after all.

I pulled the Glock from the back of my shorts' waistband. My t-shirt had covered it in the night. Starlight glinted off the barrel. "This what you're looking for?"

"You don't understand!"

"That you needed my help to cover your ass? I understand that." I didn't know if she could see me shake my head in the dark, but I did it anyway. "But you made two mistakes. One, you should have reported Paul the second you knew what he was doing to Maddy. Two, you shouldn't have decided to kill me, too. Up on the gunwale."

"Evie!" she pleaded. "Think about this." However, she did as I ordered. Maybe it was the guilt. Maybe she thought I wouldn't go through with it. She should have known better.

"I have thought about it. Every day since Maddy's funeral." I pulled the trigger once. Twice.

Kristi toppled into the black water. The speedboat

rocked as the marine predators enjoyed their extra meal. I threw the Glock into the night as far as could. I never heard the splash with the ruckus around the speedboat.

I waited an hour for the sharks to find something else to occupy their time before I lowered my kayak to the water. It took just a minute to distribute the can of gasoline over the speedboat. The smell was atrocious, and part of me regretted destroying the beautiful craft.

A quick flick of a match, a toss, and I climbed into my kayak as heat and light licked my face and hands.

I pushed away from the speedboat and checked my compass. I had paddled a mile when the heat caused the boat's fuel tank to explode. I didn't look back.

After I delivered the kayak to the guy who'd bought it through an online marketplace, I drove back to my Houston condo.

"Well, kid. It's done." I held up the suicide note, the one Maddy mailed me along with the hot pink flash drive on the afternoon she'd slit her wrists. A lick of the lighter, and black curled up the edge. I dropped the burning pink paper into the kitchen sink.

I finished washing the ashes down when the phone rang. I had been expecting the call.

"Hello?"

"Is this Evangelina Cage?"

"Yes."

"This is Detective Rodriguez with the Corpus Christi Police Department. Your brother-in-law's boat was discovered in the Gulf this morning by the Coast Guard."

"Forgive me, Detective, but why aren't you calling Paul about his boat?"

"We haven't been able to locate him or your sister." He hesitated a moment. "When was the last time you spoke with your sister?"

I resisted the urge to smile. His question meant the police had already checked the call log on Kristi's phone.

"Kristi called me yesterday about seven p.m. She'd had a fight with Paul, but they've had a lot of them over them last three months since their daughter Maddy committed suicide." I sighed. "I told her to come up to my place if things were that bad, but she didn't show up."

When Detective Rodriguez asked me to come down to Corpus Christi, I readily agreed. Of course, I was concerned about my sister. The police questioned me more thoroughly. Then Rodriguez showed me the video.

I threw up like I had the first time I watched it. Luckily, the detective had a waste can for me, so I didn't stain their carpet like I did mine.

Eventually, the investigators found a bullet embedded in a tree in the garden with Paul's blood in the hole. They surmised Kristi had found out about Paul sexually abusing Maddy and killed him before setting the boat on fire and killing herself.

Paul's family didn't want a thing to do with his estate after learning the truth. Since I was Kristi's only family, I suggested we sell all the property and donate the money to the national suicide prevention hotline in Maddy's name. Not one of them disagreed.

It took a while to wrap up the estate given the circumstances. On the first anniversary of Maddy's death, I took a bouquet of her favorite flowers to her grave. The lilacs were expensive as hell, but they were worth it. I was never coming back to Corpus Christi again.

Consequences

Every decision ever made has consequences. It's not a platitude or euphemism. People who can't think through the consequences of their decisions are caught in their own stupidity.

My decision was Dack. The consequences ended with me doing two years in the women's state penitentiary.

I should have known he was too good to be true. Sun-kissed blond hair. Chiseled cheekbones and a chin with the most adorable dimple. A lean, muscular swimmer's body. And damn, was he good between the sheets.

Even better on every other piece of furniture in what I thought was his condo.

As I contemplated my bad decision, the hot California sun pummeled the black classy dress I'd worn during my sentencing hearing as I waited outside the prison gates. Dust tickled my nose. The air had that desperate, pungent quality when it hasn't rained for ages. It was weirdly quiet outdoors after being used to the constant noise inside the cell block. Even with lights out, there was snoring, grunting, and coughing.

I kicked the little tuft of grass struggling to force its roots through the packed dirt beside the concrete walkway. The blades bent and sprang back. Not even my stilettos spoiled the plant's determination. Maybe the universe was trying to tell me something.

A tan sedan pulled up in front of me. The passenger side window lowered. Olivia, my former cell mate, leaned over and said, "You getting in, Grace, or are you taking out your attitude on more innocent plants?"

White teeth flashed a counterpoint against her dark skin. I resisted the urge to flip her off. Her assistance was crucial to my plan.

I yanked open the passenger door and slid into the seat. "You're late."

"Nope." Olivia glanced at me to make sure I'd shut the door before she executed a U-turn and guided the sedan down the driveway. Seatbelts were irrelevant in her world, which was exactly why I buckled up. "I am exactly on time."

I snorted. Our verbal routine was nothing new. "Did you find him?"

"105 Preskine Street," Olivia briskly replied. "Taking a cougar for all she's worth. He's using the name Brett." Of course, he was using a pseudonym. I had to do a lot of digging during the short periods I was allowed to use the computer while incarcerated to discover his real name.

Another consequence from my bad decision. I'd been stupid enough to give him my real name.

Olivia shot another glance at me. "This would be a whole lot easier if you just killed him."

"No." My face tightened into an ugly grin. "I want the bastard to hurt for what he did to me."

My first step was to make contact with Dack's new mark. Antoinette Case may have inherited most of her wealth, but she worked her ass off as Malibu's top real estate agent. So it didn't take much to get her attention. Especially since I kept most of my ill-gotten gains in an offshore account.

I may have given Dack my heart and my real name, but I wasn't foolish enough to give him locations and bank account numbers.

The Tuesday after my release, I walked into Case's office wearing a designer double-breasted navy suitdress with matching navy three-inch pumps and purse. She didn't question my new persona because she waltzed into the reception area of her office with her sunglasses on and keys in hand as soon as her assistant announced my presence.

"Ms. Case." I shook her hand.

"Please call me Toni, Ms. Montclair," she replied. Her artfully dyed blond hair was pulled into an elegant chignon, and she wore a pale pink pantsuit.

"Then I'm Sophie." I kept the pleasant but bored expression on my face.

"I've picked out three houses on the PCH for lease that met the requirements your assistant Olivia sent me."

"I sincerely hope one of them works," I murmured. "I'd like to wrap up the whole matter this afternoon."

Toni was smart when it came to showing properties. The third one was the best. Most of the windows faced the Pacific Ocean, including spacious views from all four bedrooms. Plenty of room to entertain, yet still small enough to feel cozy.

If I weren't in the middle of seeking revenge on the man who left me to rot in prison, this would have been a perfect place to settle down. Maybe I was getting old. This life can take its toll.

"You are good." I gave Toni a genuine smile. "I love it." I hesitated a moment, playing for her need to help others. "Once I get moved in, would you like to have dinner? I really don't know anyone on this side of the country." I waved a hand. "You know how it is when everybody just wants something from you."

"I do. I do." She nodded. "You have my contact information. And I can show you the better restaurants." She winked.

"I would love that." The trap was baited. Now, I just needed to lure in the mouse.

"Patience may be a virtue, but it's annoying as hell," Olivia complained.

We'd been living in the house for two weeks. Furnishings had arrived and been arranged. Olivia's impeccable talent as an interior decorator shone throughout the house. Too bad she'd blown her reputation by embezzling from her partner. But then, I'd agreed to split whatever I could get out of Dack from the deal he'd double-crossed me on.

"Shush." I flittered my fingers. "Go work in the den."

Olivia cocked her head. "There better be some crab salad left after she's gone." But she marched out of the kitchen. The better to stay out of my way while I worked Toni. I'd invited the real estate agent for a light supper.

And to show off Olivia's talent.

When Toni arrived, she marveled over the interior. I gave her a tour.

"I don't suppose I could get you to stage my listed properties," she asked as we re-entered the kitchen.

"I'm not that talented." I pulled the prepared plates from the huge stainless steel refrigerator. "Olivia used to be an interior decorator."

Toni waved. "I suppose it can be difficult to find a new position when you have a record."

A chill ran through me, but I forced a smile. "How did you know about her?"

"There's little things." Toni took a bite of her salad

and chewed while watching me. She swallowed and said, "Including a background check."

"Does it bother you that my assistant has a criminal past?"

She grinned. "Not any more than your stint in the slammer does. Grace."

I could have blamed my choking fit on the fresh-ground black pepper in my salad. I sipped my sparkling water. "So, what do you want? To blackmail us?"

Toni waved away my question. "Actually, I'm hoping you meant what you said about us being friends."

My hackles rose. "And what kind of friendly favor do you need?"

"My boyfriend is cheating on me with my assistant Michelle." She toyed with her napkin before she looked me directly in the eye. "I want to punish him."

***

I called Olivia back into the kitchen. She dished up her own crab salad before she sat at the breakfast bar with Toni and me.

"I don't mind the money and car." Toni shook her head. "I knew he was looking for a sugar momma. It's the cheating that bothers the heck out of me."

For a split second, I was a little jealous of Toni. She went into her relationship with her eyes wide open. I had been the idiot when it came to Dack.

"So, what do you want from us?" Olivia asked. "Cut off his dick? Kneecap him?"

"Wait." I held up my hand. I didn't know where the sudden need for honesty came from. Probably the same place as the weird feeling of regret. Was this guilt I was experiencing?

I sucked in a deep breath. "There's something you should know, Toni. I targeted you because Dack is the reason I ended up in prison."

"Dack?" She cocked her head.

"That's the name I knew him as." I laid my fork on my plate, my appetite gone. "He's a con artist."

Sympathy flitted across Toni's face. "And you lost your focus."

I nodded.

"What do you want out of this?" she asked.

"I want him to hurt."

She smiled. "And you, Olivia?"

"My deal with Grace is half the take from Dack, Brett, whoever he really is."

Someone could hit me with a feather and knocked me all the way to San Francisco. I wasn't expecting this level of honesty from Olivia.

"And what do you want out of this, Toni?" I asked.

"Same as you. I want to hurt him. If he ends up in jail, even better. But there's one other thing." She hesitated. "Can you help me prove Michelle is embezzling from my company?"

Olivia glanced at me before she nodded. "Oh, definitely."

Toni raised her sparkling water, and the three of us clinked our bottles to seal the deal.

It took us a couple of days to put together the scam. We were going to play into Dack's rather common fantasy of a threesome. He'd brought up the subject enough when we were together. I'm glad I'd never gone through with it.

No con artist trusts a bank, so the incident needed to have consequences bad enough for Dack to bolt to where his go pack rested. Since Olivia was the only one of us he hadn't met, she was elected to play Toni's kinky friend.

The two of them went to a local club for happy hour. Toni called Dack to meet them there before she left her office. I sat in the parking lot across the street and watched.

Sure enough, he pulled into the club's parking lot, driving a very expensive sports convertible. What an obvious marker. And why hadn't I seen it before?

Stupid hormones, that's why.

My wireless earbud crackled with Olivia saying, "He just entered." She'd left her phone on so I could monitor the situation.

Toni's muffled voice said, "Then you'd better lay some sugar on me."

From the sounds, they stopped their kiss long before Dack made it to their table. And as I calculated, he was intrigued by the idea of Olivia and Toni together rather than appalled. About an hour, dinner and a couple of drinks each, the trio decided to go to Toni's house for a nightcap.

Toni and Olivia rode together in Toni's little convertible. With the top down and the sun just touching the edge of the horizon, the ladies gave Dack such a good show, I don't think he even looked in his car's mirrors.

Dark clouds rolled in from the south as I parked in a neighbor's driveway, someone Toni knew was away for the weekend. It almost felt like listening to a soap opera back in the days when they were on the radio. Complete with the thunder and lightning as a dramatic backdrop.

The ladies didn't have to do much to get Dack into Toni's bedroom where Olivia proceeded to do an award-worthy performance as a woman allegedly suffering an overdose. But then, Toni's panicked response would have earned her best-supporting actress.

The first huge drops of water splattered on my windshield when a barely dressed Dack bolted out of Toni's house and leapt into his sports car. He reached the end of the drive before the idiot realized it was raining. I laughed as I watched him put up the convertible top. From the jerky motions of his head, he swore a blue streak. Once the top was secured, he whipped out of the driveway and raced down the Pacific Coast Highway. The rain picked up while I followed at a safe distance.

"We're in the car. Where's he headed?" Olivia asked in my ear.

I strained to see through the heavy splats of water. Ahead of me, he signaled to turn left. "He's turning into the Paradise Canyon Apartments."

"That's where Michelle lives," Toni growled.

"You think she's in on it?" I asked.

"It's possible," Toni admitted.

I signaled to turn into the complex. "What's her apartment number?"

The rain had slowed considerably by the time I parked Olivia's sedan. I made sure I had my fake pistol in my raincoat pocket before I grabbed the box from a certain Seattle tech giant/retail company. It was early enough in the evening their runners could still be making stops.

After I lowered the hood over my head, I jogged up to the second floor and hammered on the door. "Delivery!"

Shadows shifted in the peephole. A woman's voice shouted back, "Just leave it on the mat."

"Sorry, but I need a signature, ma'am!" I caught voices behind the door arguing, but I couldn't make out what they were saying.

Finally, the door opened. Toni's assistant looked awfully young between no makeup and her shorts and t-shirt. I shoved the box into Michelle's gut. Despite her grunt of pain, she reflexively grabbed the cardboard. I pulled my gun and shoved back my hood.

"Where is he?" I demanded.

She dropped the box on her left foot, yelled, and hopped backward with tears in her eyes. I didn't blame her. A box of magazines was pretty heavy.

I shut the door and locked it before the neighbors got nosey. "Where is he?"

"Who?" she wailed.

"Dack. Brett. Whatever name the bastard gave you." I raised the gun and pointed at the spot between her eyes. "He came in here, so where is he?"

"Don't shoot me!" Michelle cried in earnest now. "I didn't know he was seeing anyone but Toni."

"We're at the door," Olivia said in my ear.

Without taking my eyes off Michelle, I stepped back and unlocked the door. Olivia and Toni stepped inside.

"Screwing around with my boyfriend was one thing, Michelle." Toni clicked her tongue against the roof of her mouth. "But I can't tolerate you stealing from my company. However, I will ask about reduced charges if you tell us where Brett is."

Michelle sank down and perched on the arm of her couch while she massaged her bruised foot. She couldn't meet anyone's eyes. "He's in the bedroom."

"Brett, get out here, or I'll let Grace shoot you," Toni yelled.

He hesitantly entered the living room with his hands up. "Hello, Grace."

I turned the gun on him.

"Grace?" Michelle looked at me, at him, then back at me. "I thought your name was Sophie?"

"Where is it, Dack?" I demanded. "You set me up, so I want the loot."

"Guns aren't your style, Gracie."

"I'll shoot!"

"No, you won't." Dack's smile was sad, pitying. He was so damn sure of himself. So sure he knew me.

"You're right." I smiled back. "I should let Toni cut off your johnson."

He blanched at that threat. So he was more afraid of Toni. Interesting.

"It's in the crawl space over Michelle's closet," he finally said.

"Get it," Toni snapped.

"Is that smart?" Olivia whispered after he left the living room.

"He can't fit through the bathroom window, and the bedroom window is a sheer drop," Toni said.

"The only other exit is the balcony." I gestured at the sliding glass door with the gun. "He might survive that, depending on how he lands."

"Are-are you really going to kill him?" Michelle's face was pale. "Are you going to kill me?"

"No," Toni said. "The police are on their way here."

Dack walked back into the living room with a huge duffel bag. "Here's what's left."

"I want the keys to your little hotrod, too." I waggled the fingers of my left hand.

He tossed the keys, but as I reached to catch them, he swung the duffle bag at my head. I landed hard on my ass. The other women shouted. He darted for the door, and our feet tangled.

I didn't trip him on purpose. He was right. I wasn't that type.

Dack smashed headfirst into the steel railing, bounced off, and tumbled down the concrete stairs.

The four of us gathered on the landing outside Michelle's door. From the odd angle of Dack's head, his gigolo days were over.

Deputies from the Los Angeles County Sheriff's Office hauled off Michelle. The coroner's office took Dack's body. The detective in charge strongly suggested that we come down to the Malibu station to be questioned, or he would use the cuffs on us. I made sure to tell him about the fake gun in my pocket to prove I was cooperating.

Toni, Olivia, and I stuck to our rehearsed stories. As our boyfriend, Dack had conned money from Toni and me as Sophie Montclair. He then seduced Michelle into embezzling more money from Toni's real estate company. Both Toni and I had hired Olivia as a forensic accountant, and she was the one who put together that our so-called boyfriends were actually the same person.

I came to Michelle's apartment to confront Dack. Toni and Olivia followed me to keep me from doing anything stupid.

Detective Sifuentes looked up from his notes. "Threatening someone with a gun, even a fake, is assault, Ms. Montclair."

"Can we make a deal?" I lowered the ice pack the paramedic had given me for the right side of my face.

He gestured for me to continue.

"Dack, Brett, whatever his real name is." I waved my right hand. "He used Toni's assistant just like he used me. I won't press charges against her for hiding my money for him if she's willing to forgo the assault charge."

"There's still the matter of manslaughter." The detective tapped his pen against the table top.

I pointed at the bruising on my face. "How is it manslaughter when he hit me, then tripped over his own damn feet and broke his neck?"

Sifuentes snorted. "All right, Ms. Montclair. That's all the questions I have. For now."

I left the interrogation room and found Toni and Olivia in the waiting area. A glance at the clock on the wall said it was after three in the morning.

"Holy crap!" Olivia whistled. "You are going to have one hell of a shiner."

"Tell me about it," I grumbled.

We walked out of the police station. The storm had cleared, but ozone still sharpened the air.

"Olivia, why don't you drive my car back to my place?" Toni handed her the keys. "I'll take Sophie. That way we can take turns keeping an eye on her."

"I don't need anyone—" I started to protest.

"Then you should have let the paramedics check out your head," Toni shot back.

In the end, I agreed. I really didn't want to be alone tonight. Not after the way Dack's dead eyes had stared at me from the bottom of the steps at Michelle's apartment.

None of us could sleep when we got to Toni's house. She mixed cocktails for her and Olivia and cracked open a diet soda for me. Once we were settled on her giant white sectional, Toni grinned.

"Tonight was fun despite Brett or Dack's plunge down the stairs. And we do make a great team." She sipped her Manhattan before she eyed me. "What's the next target, boss?"

No Regrets

A technicality.

A goddamned technicality.

After everything my former co-worker Lewis Anderson put me through, the bastard was going to walk out of the courtroom without even a slap on the wrist.

The DA turned to me. "I'm so sorry, Kay."

At the defendant's table, Anderson smirked at me.

Papers rattled as the attorneys collected their documents and shoved them back in their briefcases. Instead of icy fingers of fear, a white-hot blister of rage swelled within me.

I'd lost my left eye the night he threw acid at me. A ton of medical bills were piled on my kitchen table. I'd been fired from my job thanks to that bastard's lies. I was about to lose my house. I had nothing left.

Nothing but the pain and the rage festering.

My fingers touched the network of scar tissue on the left side of my face. Something evil gleamed in his eyes. Something that cut through the numbness to the blister inside me. That was when I broke and the poison filled me.

Anderson made a point of walking past me toward the exit. He leaned close and whispered, "See you soon, love."

Where his sinister tone would have sent me into a panic attack before his trial, it hardened and tempered the molten rage. I had nothing else left, so I'd be ready for him.

I'd spent quite a bit of time studying how human psychopaths hunted. Some used bait or lures depending on who they hunted. Others simply took who they wanted because their victims hit a certain type. Then there were those like Anderson who enjoyed the fear. Those people, usually male, would drag out the chase for as long as possible. His anticipation gave me a couple of days to prepare.

In all cases, there was always more than one victim. I had no illusion I was the first woman Anderson had targeted. And I knew all the other women were dead.

First, I convinced my cousin Bill to let me test drive trade-ins at his used car lot. I took them before he put the dealer plates on and used them to follow Anderson to and from work with running a few errands in between.

Our state didn't require a license to purchase a

crossbow. I practiced at a shooting range while I knew Anderson was at work.

After the acid incident, he was given the opportunity to resign rather than be fired, a luxury I was not afforded because I foolishly went to human resources, thinking I would get help. A friend of Anderson's got him a position at another software company.

After work, he went straight home unless he stopped at a grocery store or a drive-thru for dinner. Through binoculars, I watched him eat with the TV on. Then he'd take a nap on his couch until midnight.

From the way he'd jerk awake, he had an alarm set. He'd get up from the couch and dress in black. I followed him to my neighborhood the first night. He did a slow drive by my house, but he didn't stop.

The second night, he parked in front of my house for an hour before driving off. Was he waiting to see if I noticed him outside? Or if any of the neighbors noticed?

The third night, I didn't bother waiting at his house. I parked on the street behind mine and climbed the ancient maple in my backyard. I didn't think he would make his move tonight. Something said he wanted to taunt me, whip me into a frenzy, before he actually assaulted me.

Sure enough around one in the morning, a dark figure crept around the house and peeked into my bedroom window. Of course, I hadn't slept in there since the acid attack. He watched the wig and pillows I'd arranged to make it look like someone slept in there for almost two hours before he pressed something against the window and left.

I waited a couple of hours before I climbed down and returned to the trade-in. I drove to my old employer's parking garage. The gate responded to the card I'd taken right before I was escorted from the premises. My back door into the company's system allowed me to activate it and hide the records from the other software engineers. But this was the only place I felt safe because no one would dream of looking for me here.

After climbing into the back seat, I set my alarm, huddled under a blanket, and wondered if the universe would grant me the luxury of sleep tonight.

After a few measly hours of semi-rest, I returned home and did the obvious thing. I called the police. Officer Martin responded to the call, the same officer who'd responded every other time I called. I escorted him to my bedroom. He went through the back door where he gathered the ugly note and placed it in an evidence bag.

"I'll turn this over to the detective and see if I can get it fingerprinted." But he shook his head as he spoke.

"You're not going to find any." I sniffed as if I were holding back tears. "You never do."

After Officer Martin left, I considered my next option. I had given the police an opportunity to arrest Anderson.

Therefore, time for me to take direct action. He would definitely return tonight.

~

I didn't bother following him. Instead, I went to my favorite restaurant and ordered fillet mignon. This would be my last chance for real steak.

Shortly after sundown, I slung the crossbow over my shoulder and climbed the maple.

And waited.

No dark figure came.

Not at one a.m. Not at two.

Eventually, the sun rose. I climbed down and walked in a random pattern until I reached the pickup I'd borrowed from Bill. I drove to his used car lot and traded it for a small sedan.

"You okay?" he asked.

"Fine. Why?"

"You have a crossbow," he said.

I smiled. "Target practice eases my stress.

~

On the fifth night, I took up my post in the tree. Anderson didn't make me wait. He arrived promptly at one a.m. First, he tried my bedroom window, but it was locked.

He crept to the back door.

I fired the first bolt. Anderson yelled a few obscenities

and grabbed at the wood sticking out of his calf. The loss of my eye was throwing off my depth perception.

"Not used to women fighting back?" I yelled.

"Bitch!" He yanked out the shaft. "You're going to pay for that!" He charged across the yard and started climbing the tree.

I calmly reloaded the crossbow. My second shot missed entirely. The branches creaked under his weight as he made his way to the crook where I perched.

There had been a leader during the Revolutionary War whose rallying cry was something about not shooting until his men could see the white part of an enemy's eyes. I reloaded and waited until he was below me and reaching for my right foot.

I fired.

And sat in the tree for the rest of the night, half-afraid Anderson was playing dead.

At dawn, I climbed down and went inside my house. I called the police. They arrived while I ate my English muffin and drank a cup of tea.

Bill and his wife offered to pay for an attorney, but I told them to save their money and that I loved them both. I signed my confession against my public defender's advice. At my arraignment, I pled guilty. Also against my defender's advice. I just needed everything to be over.

Since I pled guilty to first degree murder, I only faced

the sentencing hearing. Bless his heart, my defender actually tried to get me a lighter sentence after he failed to get the judge to declare me incompetent.

On that morning, the judge looked at me. "Ms. Larsen, do you wish to make a statement before sentencing?"

I stood. "Yes, Your Honor." I glanced at the card my public defender had written out for me. It was all lies. I was so tired of the lies. Especially the lies our society tells itself.

Meeting the judge's gaze, I took a deep calming breath. "Your Honor, my only regret is not acting sooner. If I'd killed Lewis Anderson before the night in my yard, I would have saved more women's lives."

The press and gallery exploded. The judge hammered his gavel. When the courtroom finally quieted, he looked at me with a sad expression.

"Given her lack of remorse, I sentence the defendant to life without parole."

Two years later, I sat in the common room of the state penitentiary, playing cards with my cellmate and a couple of other women when "Special Report" flashed across the TV screen.

Apparently when the city went to tear down the house where Lewis Anderson had grown up, the wrecking crew had discovered bodies. Four women. Tortured. Murdered.

My cellmate turned to me. "Isn't that guy the reason you're here?"

"Yeah." I looked at the discard pile.

One of the other woman muttered, "Shit. You could have ended up in that basement."

"That was his intent." I checked my hand again, then picked up the top card of the pile.

"I ain't never killed anyone," the fourth woman murmured. "You ever regret it?"

"I'm alive. So are all the other women he would have targeted." I smiled. "So, no. I have no regrets." I laid down my cards. "Rummy."

In the Pale Moonlight

"Why can't we get beignets in the morning?" I protested. Sweat and humidity drenched even my underwear in the hot summer night. Things were starting to chafe. I wanted nothing more than to crank up the A/C in our hotel room and shower no matter how tempting the odor of fried dough, powdered sugar, and chicory coffee were.

"Because I always celebrate a successful job in this city with beignets." Charlee threaded her dainty white fingers through mine and dragged me in the direction of Café Du Monde. I swear my wife was obsessed with the place far beyond a celebratory eatery. On the other hand, I could never say no to her.

The French Quarter vibrated with music and laughter. Hell, the revelers were just getting started at one a.m. The crowds weren't as insane as Mardi Gras, but they came pretty damn close.

Close enough, I grabbed the kid who slipped his hand into Charlee's purse the same time she did.

The purse was a distraction, just like my wallet was.

Neither of us kept anything valuable in them. We'd both been on the streets long enough we knew better.

Surprisingly, the kid we grabbed grinned up at us. He couldn't have been more than nine or ten. Clean, too.

"Y'all are as good as they say," he murmured with a thick Cajun accent. "The note I was supposed to leave is your purse, ma'am."

Charlee reached in her purse and drew out a scrap of white, lined notebook paper. She frowned as she read the note before she looked at me. "Let him go."

I released the kid. He had the nerve to hold out his hand.

"Tip?" he said with an impish smile.

"You're damn lucky I don't whoop your ass for such a sloppy picking job."

He flipped me off before he dived back through the crowd and was lost.

I turned back to Charlee. "What was that all about?"

"Why don't you go back to our hotel room and get that shower you wanted?" She smiled up at me, but after all our years together, I knew she was faking it. "I'll get my beignets and meet you there."

I wasn't worried about leaving her alone on the streets of New Orleans in the wee hours. Charlee could more than take care of herself. But someone paid the kid to deliver a message to her, and that bugged the hell out of me.

"Let me see it."

She stuck her tongue out at me, but she handed over the piece of paper.

Of course, the damn note was written in French. Or I thought it was. I wasn't too sure. I glared at her before I handed it back.

"So who are we meeting and why?" I demanded.

"There's no 'we' here, honey." She glared right back. "This isn't any of your concern."

"If it involves you, it's my concern," I growled.

Her nostrils flared as she exhaled. I knew how weird it sounded, but I was never more turned on than when I exasperated her.

"You'll follow me if I don't invite you along." She tapped her right toe against the cobblestone. The hot pink high tops stood out despite the surrounding neon lights.

I didn't bother to answer. She already knew I would.

"Fine," she finally said. "But I do all the talking."

～

After a taxi ride to the east side, Charlee led me into what used to be the city's Lower Ninth Ward. Storm surge and levee breaks from Hurricane Katrina didn't just flood the area. They smashed the homes and businesses into piles of scrap. Decades later, the place still looked like a war zone. Rumors said people occasionally stumbled upon human remains after all this time.

I looked around us. No lights other than the glow

from the rest of the city and the pale crescent moon just above the dark shadows of the ruins. Yeah, we were in the middle of a perfect setting for a zombie movie. The hairs on the back of my neck rose. Someone was definitely watching us. But I kept my promise to keep my trap shut and didn't point this out to Charlee.

She stopped in the middle of what may have been a tiny alley years ago, raised her fingers to her lips. Her piercing whistle rent the silence. Figures emerged from the rubble in front of us.

On both sides.

Behind us.

Yep, we were trapped in a Romero nightmare.

"You came," one of the shambling figures in front of us said. Like the kid in the Quarter, he had a Cajun accent. As he came closer, I realized he used a cane.

I felt Charlee's tenseness at this meeting, but it wasn't like she suspected we were in danger. No, it was more like her attitude when something from her past came up. She wasn't comfortable, but she wasn't going to run away either. Maybe we weren't looking at our imminent deaths after all.

"You knew I would," Charlee replied coolly. "What do you want, Marquis?"

"One of my protégés has been taken."

When she spoke, her words carried a load of bitterness. "You can't keep someone a child forever—"

"She didn't walk away from me," Marquis said. "She was kidnapped."

"No one in the city would touch one of yours," Charlee said. "So spill."

"They are two brothers from Miami. Gillian's parents have been offering a one million-dollar reward for her safe return."

I whistled. The heat from Charlee's glare could have incinerated me in this darkness.

"C'mon, babe." I gestured at the man in front of us. "You got to be askin' yourself. Why didn't he collect?"

"She was a runaway," Charlee murmured. "He's not going to stab one of his trainees in the back."

"It sets a bad precedent," Marquis added.

"So these boys from Miami spotted her on the street?" I kind of wished I'd pushed my wife about the details while we were in the cab. I didn't get a good feeling about this Marquis.

"Unfortunately." He tapped his cane on the broken asphalt. "They are now attempting to extort more money from her parents and threatening to kill her if they do not comply."

"Why do you need me?" Charlee's voice deepened with anger. Even I knew better than to mess with her when she was this pissed.

"It's the Cedano brothers."

A gasp escaped from my throat. The Cedanos were known enforcers with the Mateo Cartel. They were smart, vicious, and didn't often leave survivors. At least, not on purpose. Even I knew better than to spark their attention.

"What the hell are they doing in New Orleans?" I snapped. Because God knew it couldn't be good.

"They arrived to pick up a package for their boss. A present for his daughter. She's getting married next month." Marquis exhaled. "Then they decided to become tourists."

"They haven't tried you for the money?" Charlee crossed her arms over her chest.

"If they know she's one of mine, they are playing it close to their chest. If you plan to offer your assistance, may we go somewhere more pleasant to continue this discussion?"

I looked down at my wife. Her blond hair appeared silver under the moonlight. She had the blank look she got when she calculated the odds.

"How old?" she finally said.

"Eleven."

That's when I knew we were screwed.

❧

Marquis and two of his people led us to the Upper 9th Ward where renovation and reconstruction had started for the lots with a clear title. The rest of them disappeared into the rubble once again.

We entered an understated but clean shotgun house.

The door to the bedroom was closed, but that didn't block the snoring.

Marquis turned out to be an elderly Black gentleman. One of his men was white, the other mixed.

"Have a seat." Marquis gestured at the couch lining one wall. However, his Cajun accent disappeared. Now, he sounded like an Ivy League English professor. "Would you two care for a drink?"

"No, thank you, sir," I replied politely.

"Bottled water," Charlee said, but her eyes narrowed. Almost as if she dared Marquis to argue with her.

The white lackey opened the door of what appeared to be an antique credenza. Instead, it disguised a mini-fridge. He pulled out a bottle, closed the fridge door, and brought the water to Charlee. I almost wanted to ask for one of the longnecks inside the mini-fridge, but a beer was the last thing I needed when I was this tired and negotiating with New Orleans' Master of Thieves.

At least, the minion didn't stand over us or hold up the wall. He sat in the rocking chair while Marquis lowered himself into an old recliner. The other minion sat on a nearby ottoman and played with the cat who'd been sleeping on the recliner when we walked into the house.

Charlee cracked open the seal and said, "How'd a rich white kid end up with you?" She swigged a quarter of the bottle without taking her eyes off Marquis.

"Sweetheart, I'm sorry I hurt your feelings all those years ago." He shook his head. "But a blond, white girl living with a Black family would've raised too many questions with the authorities." He eyed me. "Is that why you chose this young gentleman as your partner? To get what you thought I deprived you of?"

"If you mean a family of her own, then yes, she did," I said evenly as I interlocked my fingers with hers. I wasn't about to put up with anybody second-guessing my relationship with my wife. Least of all, someone who rejected her. "And since I am her partner in all ways, I suggest you be straight with us, or we're walking."

Marquis nodded sharply and smiled. "Good. She's going to need your assistance." He pulled out a sheet of paper from the pile of junk mail on the end table between his recliner and the couch and handed it to Charlee.

"Gillian ran away from her parents last year." Marquis pointed at the white lackey. "Beau here found her. Charlee can tell you we try to get the younger children off the streets before the pimps find them."

She handed me the paper. It was a typical missing child poster. Recent photograph. A plea for information of the child's whereabouts. Phone number to call with information. I looked up at Marquis.

"It mentions a cash reward, but this doesn't say a damn thing about the amount," I pointed out. "It could be a dollar as far as anyone knows. Where'd you get the million dollar figure?"

"A friend on the NOLA police force," he said. "Gillian's

parents own a construction company. They got a lot of the contracts for rebuilding after Katrina—"

"And made a ton of money," Charlee finished.

Marquis nodded. "Their two older children work for them. Gillian was a surprise pregnancy." He leaned his elbows on the recliner's armrests and folded his fingers together.

I focused on his hands. The joints were swollen, but otherwise his digits had the slender, uncalloused build of a pianist.

Or a lock pick.

"—neglect can be worse than outright abuse," Marquis was saying.

"But what about mixing?" Charlee sneered.

Instead of Marquis, it was Beau who answered. "Does Jasper here look like my brother? Well, he is my blood. Times are changing, Miz Charlee. Your man and my brother are proof of that. So quit harping on Marquis because you didn't get your way as a little girl!"

The snoring halted for a second. Everyone in the living room froze, including me. Mumbling came from behind the closed door, then the snoring resumed.

"Is that Miz Martha?" Charlee asked softly.

Marquis nodded. "She isn't well. Cancer."

The pain in Charlee's face shocked me. She rarely spoke about any time before we met. But she obviously cared a great deal for the person snoring in the bedroom.

"How bad?" she finally asked.

"Stage four."

Her face hardened. The same look she got when she compartmentalized her emotions. "Do you know where the Cedano brothers are keeping Gillian?"

Again, Marquis nodded.

"Here's the deal." She waved her hand to include me. "We get her out of the Cedanos' clutches. We get them arrested. We return her to her parents—"

"So you can get the reward money." Turned out that Beau could sneer even better than my wife.

"Nope." Charlee shook her head. "The money will go into a trust to assist people in the Ninth Ward to rebuild their homes."

"A million isn't going to go far," Jasper said sadly.

"We'll throw a little into the pot," I said.

"And we'll negotiate Gillian being allowed to visit Miz Martha," Charlee finished. "Her parents don't have to know anymore than that."

"I hate losing her." Marquis's eyes glittered, but I wasn't sure with what emotion. I was usually a lot better at reading people, but I couldn't tell if he was pissed or pleased by Charlee's proposal.

"That's the only offer you'll get from me," Charlee stated.

After a long moment, Marquis nodded sharply once. "Done."

Two hours later, I stepped out of the shower with a towel around my waist. Not even the A/C cranked up on high and the cool water made me feel less sweaty. Charlee hadn't moved from the desk in the corner of our hotel room. Papers were spread across the surface, but one bag of beignets was gone.

I grabbed the second bag and sat on the corner of the bed "You need to come clean with me, baby. You know I respect your privacy, but I don't like the feeling I'm getting from this Marquis."

"You don't have to be involved." She looked up at me, but it wasn't anger or irritation. It was the worried expression she got when she thought I was in over my head. "This is my debt, not yours."

"You know that's not how we roll," I snapped. "We're a team. Forever. What do you owe Marquis?"

"I don't owe him," she said softly. "I owe Miz Martha."

"Baby, you need to start your story from the beginning." I wanted to pull her in my arms and tell her everything would be all right. However, Charlee was wired differently than any woman I'd ever met. It was one of the things I adored about her.

I also knew if I touched her now, she'd bolt, and I'd never know what the hell was going on.

"I tried to pick Miz Martha's purse." Charlee's voice sounded terribly small, like that of a ten-year-old girl. "It was my first time, and I was so hungry. Instead of calling the police, she took me home with her."

My wife looked at me with tears in her eyes. It shocked me. Charlee wasn't a crier.

"They taught me so much." She swallowed hard. "I wanted them to adopt me. Instead, Marquis sent me to a friend of his, Montague."

"He pimped you?" It was all I could do to leave my fingers loose and resting on my terry-covered thighs when I wanted to beat the stuffing out of this Marquis.

"No." She smiled. "Montague wasn't into women, much less children. He was the best thief of his generation. And at the age of eleven, I was the best of mine. He was looking for someone to pass on his knowledge to. An heir. Not an apprentice. Not a protégé. And definitely not a daughter."

"But what about Marquis?" I asked. "Do you trust him?"

"No." Her jaw worked a few times before she added, "He's the seller the Cedanos were to meet here in New Orleans."

That observation jolted me. "How do you know that?"

This time, her usual smirk appeared on her face. "The way he kept emphasizing honor among thieves. But the Cedanos aren't thieves."

No, they definitely weren't. So why would the cartel send them? "You think they pulled a fast one on Marquis?"

Charlee nodded. "And Marquis retaliated, so they grabbed Gillian as compensation."

I cocked my head trying to work out the tangle. "But the Cedanos are extorting money from Gillian's parents."

"So whatever they were supposed to pick up from Marquis is worth more than a million." Charlee shrugged. "They can't go back to Miami empty-handed."

"What about Miz Martha?"

Charlee's expression darkened. "Regardless of her husband, she'd never forgive me if anything happened to that little girl."

The only reason I got Charlee to sleep was we both needed to be fresh for our plan.

It didn't take a whole lot of digging to learn Gillian's parents were Kent and Callista LaFontaine. And yeah, the million dollar reward for Gillian would be nothing to them.

While Charlee scouted the building in the CBD where Marquis said the Cedano brothers were holed up with Gillian, I requisitioned the supplies we would need to extract the girl.

Getting into the building wasn't the problem. Getting out without anyone dying would be. I had no illusions of how dangerous the brothers were.

The Cedanos were staying at an exclusive condo owned by the Miami cartel. Luckily, an heiress on the same floor was having a huge birthday party. It only took a few minutes to forge invitations for me and Charlee.

We borrowed a condo on the floor below the Cedanos and the party for our prep area. While Charlee cased the building, disguised as part of the cleaning staff, she learned the owners were in Europe for the month.

The nice thing about black-tie affairs is the waitstaff are dressed similarly to the male guests. I could wear any old penguin suit.

Charlee, however, had to dress the part of an heiress's friend. When she stepped out of the master bathroom in the blue silk sheath, I whistled. She shot me a double-bird before she turned to double-check her hair and makeup in the dresser mirror.

I couldn't help it. She looked damn fine in that dress. It clung to her curves in all the right ways. I wanted to slowly pull it off, kissing her skin every step of the way.

Charlee's reflection glared at me. "Baby, we don't have time for that kind of crap."

"Since when is making love to my wife crap?" I feigned offense.

"When a little girl's life is on the line," she snapped.

A bucket of ice water couldn't have chilled my ardor the way her words did. She viewed any other job as a hobby, the way other women saw gardening or knitting or book clubs. But when it came to kids . . . well, her childhood was shittier than mine. Her purpose in life was to help children in trouble.

And Gillian was definitely in deep, deep trouble.

Five minutes later, we rode the elevator up to the sixth floor. Not only did music fill the air, the bass from an expensive sound system rattled the floor and my teeth. Charlee and I laughed loudly as we approached Unit 615. I banged on the door.

It opened a crack, enough I could make out an eye behind the chain on the door.

"Go away," Raphael Cedano growled.

"Come on, Victor," Charlee whined like a slightly buzzed upper class party girl. "Don't be a putz. It's Laura's birthday."

"I'm not Victor," Raphael spat.

"Sweetie." I tugged on her elbow. "I told you 615 wasn't the right condo."

"Oops." Charlee giggled. "It sounds like you could use a drink more than me, Not-Victor. You wanna be my plus one?"

In response, he slammed the door shut. Charlee tilted her head slightly to the left, which meant she didn't see Raphael's brother in the condo either. We needed to figure out where the other Cedano was before we could make our next move. I steered my still giggling wife towards Unit 618 and knocked.

At six-two, I wasn't exactly short by any means, but the brother who answered the door had me by an easy eight inches. "Invitations," he demanded.

I produced our forged invitations from my jacket

pocket and handed them over. He glanced at the white cardboard with the gold embossing before he handed them back.

"Have a nice time," he rumbled while he stepped out of the way so we could enter.

As we walked in, I understood why there was no longer a Unit 616 listed for the building though the door for it still existed. Lauren Biggs, the heiress to Biggs Shipping, lived up to her name. The corner condo had been turned into a giant party room with the huge floor-to-ceiling windows as the backdrop. Outside, lights of the city winked at the dark hulks floating up and down the river.

What had been the next-door-condo had been subsumed into the service of the party room. Also, a spiral staircase led to the seventh floor, which meant that condo had also been appropriated by Ms. Biggs.

Waitstaff trotted back and forth from the kitchen with platters of hors d'oeuvres. They had the fishy whiff of caviar. Fish eggs was one of the things Charlee and I agreed on—caviar was disgusting, and the more it cost, the nastier it was.

A young man, who could easily be my son, held out a tray of the crap to me. This was fucking New Orleans, the home of some of the best seafood in the world, but these were the type of people who looked down at excellent crawfish gumbo. So I played the rich asshole and gagged down the caviar on a toast point. Thank god, the excellent champagne another waitress brought over to us washed away the taste.

We approached Lauren who perched on a large chair in the corner where the wall-sized windows met. A chair large enough and styled to be throne-like. However, it was the man sitting next to her on a normal chair that caused a split-second of hesitation.

Gabriel Cedano.

Now, why the hell was he here? However, it did explain Raphael's pissy attitude. I wouldn't want to be stuck babysitting my kidnap victim when there was a party next door.

"Lauren, darling!" Charlee charged forward and air-kissed the heiress. "Happy birthday!"

"I'm so glad you came!"

I had to give Lauren credit for her excellent acting skills. She didn't have a clue of who we were.

"Happy Birthday, sexy." I took Lauren's left hand and brought the back to my lips. She blushed at my flirty behavior. "Glad business brought us to town in time for your celebration."

"You have a new deal going on?" Lauren smiled.

"Just a little art acquisition." Charlee smirked as she smacked my chest. "You know how Adrian is always looking for those one of a kind art pieces."

From Gabriel's slight flinch, Charlee's fishing expedition had landed a whopper.

"So what do you do, Adrian?" he asked politely.

"Whatever I want these days." I grinned. "I thought I was done after I blew out my knee, but Glenda here turned my measly two million from the NFL into a stock market bonanza." I wrapped my left arm around Charlee and squeezed.

She rested her right hand on her chest. "Honey, it was Lauren's tip."

Another couple approached, which gave us our cue to exit.

"Talk to you later, sexy." I winked at Lauren.

"Well?" Charlee whispered after we circulated and pretended to know the people in the room. Her obsession with reality TV was coming in handy. "Now, we know where each brother is. Can you keep Gabriel here while I retrieve—" Her pleasant face fell for a split-second before she recovered. "Shit."

I knew better than to look behind me. "Who?"

"Kent and Callista LaFontaine just walked in. He has a briefcase with him."

"Why would they come to a party when—" My expression probably matched Charlee's. "This is the drop," I muttered.

"Do we let it go through?"

"What would you do if the kid you kidnapped and their parents saw your face?"

Charlee's eyes narrowed. "Double shit."

"Yeah, this just made our job harder."

"Not if we ignore the parents," she murmured.

"What if that's Marquis's plan?"

"Triple shit." So maybe my wife wasn't taking her mentor at face value after all. If the LaFontaines died tonight, Gillian would inherit a third of their wealth. All it would take is a couple of well-planned accidents to get rid of the kid's older siblings. Beau steps in as a distant cousin of Gillian's to become her guardian, and voila! Marquis has control of one of the largest contractors in New Orleans.

"He's playing the long con," I whispered. "He'll gentrify the entire Ninth Ward."

"Miz Martha wouldn't go along with this plan," Charlee protested. "Not if it involved murder."

"Baby, she may not be aware if she has stage four cancer."

Charlee turned toward the view of the city and closed her eyes. "I'm too close. You need to take over." For my wife to admit she was emotionally compromised indicated just how bad the situation was.

I scanned the crowd. "We're going to switch roles. Can you keep Gabriel occupied?"

She nodded. "How long?"

"Downstairs in ten minutes," I said.

Within five seconds, she had the cartel enforcer out on the balcony. She knew how to work it when someone's life was at stake.

With Gabriel out of the way, I intercepted Gillian's parents and slung an arm around each of them. "Kent! Callista! Long time, no see!"

They both stiffened under my touch. "Who the hell–" Kent started.

"Shut up and listen," I growled under my breath. "You're being set up."

"Who are you?" Callista's wide eyes were due more to plastic surgery than fear, but the way she shook under my arm, there was a healthy amount of anxiety.

"A recovery specialist hired to free your daughter," I said. "If you give the kidnappers the money they demanded, I guarantee they will kill her. She's seen their faces."

"Who hired you?" Kent demanded.

"My wife's foster mom," I said softly. "She took in Gillian when she found her on the streets. Unfortunately, a couple of goons recognized your daughter from the reward posters and snatched her." I gently squeezed their shoulders. "If you want your daughter back alive, I need you to leave now."

"Where is she?" Callista's eyes shimmered with unshed tears.

Damn. They weren't going to leave unless I could give them some kind of guarantee.

"Go downstairs," I said. "Unit 502. The entry number is four-three-seven-five. We'll bring Gillian there as soon as we have her."

A million questions crossed both of their faces. Finally, they looked at each other before they turned back to me and nodded.

"Go." I breathed a little prayer to Saint Jude when they headed for the front door. If the LaFontaines listened to me, Charlee and I had a chance to make this insane rescue work.

Once they were clear of Lauren's condo, I strode into the kitchen. Most of the workers inside only gave me the briefest of glances. However, a white man in a navy blazer and tan pants made a beeline for me.

"May I help you?" His supercilious air was annoying as hell, but I knew what would help.

I pulled out a money clip. "Can I borrow one of your stainless steel food service carts? My wife has a surprise for Lauren, and I need to sneak it up here without any of the other guests seeing."

He eyed the money clip. "Sir, you're asking to use a very expensive piece of equipment."

I peeled off a couple of benjamins. "I just need it for ten minutes."

He jutted his chin at the money clip. "Another bill and you can take your time."

Most people don't get the con game. We hook you by giving you your heart's desire. For most people, like the catering manager, it boils down to pure and simple greed.

I handed him the money. He slipped it in his front jacket pocket before he ordered the kid who could have been a younger me to clear the trays out of one of the unit.

"I can do it." I stepped closer to the manager.

"No, no, sir. He'll take care of it." He gently pushed me back, so I plucked the money I'd just given to him from his pocket.

When the manager stalked across the kitchen to yell at one of the waitresses, I held out the money to the kid.

He glanced at the bills, then looked me in the eye. "How do I know you won't pick my pocket if I accept?"

"I don't steal from a brother."

Apparently that statement was enough. He grinned, accepted the money, and slid the benjamins into his sock. In two seconds, he emptied the service cart. "There you go, sir."

"Thank you very much." I slipped off my jacket, laid it on the bottom of the cart and closed the door. No one else paid attention while I rolled the cart out the kitchen door and into the condominium hallway.

I freely admit Charlee is the brawn of our team, but I was willing to step back as the brains because this job was so important to her. Now, I had to be both, or three people were going to die tonight.

And my wife would make me the fourth if Gillian was one of the dead.

Unfortunately, it also meant banging up the cart that cost in the mid-four figures, but it had enough weight for my purpose. I rolled it down so it was positioned across the wide hallway from Unit 615. I knocked on the door before I got behind the cart.

The instant Raphael Cedano twisted the doorknob,

I rammed the heavy cart into the door. The party noise hid the bang of the cart against the door, the snap of the chain breaking, and the squeal of pain from the cartel enforcer.

I continued running and rolled the cart over Raphael. A quick flip of a switch locked the wheels. Closing the door, I glared at the enforcer. "Where is it?"

"Whad? Who?" From the angle of his nose, I'd broken it. He shoved ineffectually at the cart.

I knelt next to him. "Raphael, the boss is not happy with you and your brother for not getting his merchandise. Where is it?"

The enforcer closed his eyes. Through gritted teeth, he said, "Marquis still has it."

I narrowed my eyes. "What the fuck did you two idiots do?"

Raphael's eyes opened. "He refused to hand it over. I wanted to kill him and take the statue, but Marquis offered us a girl."

Oh, god. Charlee would blow a gasket when she found out her old mentor had lied to her.

"Jesus Christ!" I yelled and stood up. "You pissed off the boss for a piece of ass!"

"What? No!" He struggled with the cart and started to wheeze. The cart sat on his chest, and he was slowly suffocating, but he wasn't in danger yet. "She's . . . an . . . heiress . . . reward."

I rubbed my lower jaw like I was considering what to do next. "Have you collected?"

White appeared around Raphael's nearly black irises. Brother's . . . make . . . making . . . exchange."

"You're lying, Raphael."

His eyes darted in the direction of the hallway leading to the second and third bedrooms. I pulled out the zip ties that hung from a special loop inside my slacks. It took a minute to search what I could on his person and secure his wrists and ankles.

I headed down the hall, but first, I locked his handgun and switchblade in the half bath. It wasn't much of a lock. I just needed time to get out of here with Gillian.

The kid was in the third bedroom. She could have been Charlee at the same age. Pale blonde hair and huge blue eyes. She inhaled to scream, but all the duct tape over her mouth muffled the sound.

I laid a finger over my lips. She blinked.

"Miz Martha sent me," I whispered. "She's pissed about what Marquis did to you. I really need you to be quiet while I get you out of here."

Gillian nodded.

I winced as I peeled off the duct tape from her face. "I'm really sorry for hurting you."

"I want my mom." Her voice was feather-quiet, but fat tears rolled down her cheeks.

"We'll take you to her."

She froze for a second when I pulled a mini box cutter from my pocket.

I held up my hands. "I need to cut off the rest of the tape. I couldn't cut it off your face without hurting you."

Gillian nodded in jerky motions.

I quickly cut her free. Once I pocketed my knife, she clung to my right hand as if it were a life preserver. We entered the condo's living room, and Gillian pressed against my body.

"You . . . can't . . . leave . . . me . . ." Raphael's fingers were turning an interesting bluish purple.

"We don't deal in children," I growled, which was true for both me and Charlee as well as the Mateo Cartel. I unlocked the wheels and deliberated jerked the cart over his junk. Raphael's scream was higher pitched than my wife's, and I'd only ever heard her scream once.

"Get inside, Gillian," I said.

The girl hesitated and glanced at me before she climbed inside and pulled the door shut.

I opened the door and rolled the cart into the hallway. No one was out here. I closed the door of Unit 615 and pushed the cart to the elevator.

The debate of what to do next consumed me. I stabbed the down button. Gillian's parents weren't innocent by any means. They screwed over Marquis in some way. Otherwise, he wouldn't have set them up to be murdered. How did Charlee and I fix this without sacrificing a child, much less our own skins?

I pushed the cart into the elevator. First step was finding out what the hell the LaFontaines did to Marquis. And the guilty parties should be in our borrowed condo right now.

Probably alone with my wife.

Getting lucky again, no one was around when we reached the fifth floor. I wheeled the cart with Gillian to our borrowed condo and entered the code into the keypad. However, upon opening the door, I discovered Kent LaFontaine aiming a gun at my wife, who sat on the couch. From the scuff marks on the carpet, Callista had been pacing while they waited for me.

"Get in here," he snapped.

I shouldn't have been surprised. I shoved the cart into the condo's living area and shut the front door. "What did you do to screw over Marquis?"

Callista blinked in surprise, but Kent's face hardened.

"None of your damn business," he snapped.

"It was bad enough he put Gillian in danger, and he set up a Miami cartel team to kill you and your wife," I said calmly.

Callista turned to her husband. "What is he talking about, Kent?"

"A proposed business deal," he said coolly. "It fell through, but one of the partners blames me."

"Tell your wife the truth, Kent," I said. "You double-crossed the man who controls half the New Orleans underworld."

Callista and Charlee both stared at Kent. Red flushed his skin, and he tugged at his necktie.

Charlee looked back at me. Her eyes sparked with her fury over her old mentor setting her up, too.

"You-you put our daughter's life in danger over a fucking business deal?" Callista shrieked.

"Where is Gillian?" Kent demanded.

I knocked on the top of the service cart. The side door rolled up and Gillian crawled out. She immediately ran to her mom.

Charlee ignored the gun aimed at her. "What if we tell the Cedano brothers the truth?"

"That Kent and Marquis were using them in their pissing contest?" I chuckled. "That's a good way for everyone to end up dead."

"You won't be telling anyone anything," Kent said.

"Oh, put that thing away," Callista snapped as she cuddled Gillian. "No one's killing anyone. And give them the damn money for getting our baby back."

"You said Miz Martha sent you." The girl gave me an accusing glare.

"She did," Charlee said. "She looked out for me when I was your age. She trusted my husband and I would get you back safe and sound."

"See?" Kent waved his gun in my general direction. "They're just going to give our money to the people who kept our daughter from us. These two are part of the kidnapping."

Gillian stepped away from her mom. I'd never seen a preteen with such an expression of rage. "No one took me! I ran away because your stupid company is more important to you than me!"

"Wh-what are you talking about?" Callista wore an appalled look.

"Why don't you ask Dad?" The girl shook with the power of her anger. "He said he'd be glad when I pulled my own weight around the house and made him some money."

"Is this true?" Callista started to reflect her daughter's anger.

"They're criminals!" Kent's contemptuous handling of his firearm was beginning to make me nervous. "They're lying."

"Actually, we're confidential specialists," Charlee said. "We perform services for people who need discretion."

"And if you kill us, I guarantee every one of your dirty secrets will be all over the internet by tomorrow morning." I crossed my arms.

"You're bluffing." Kent sneered in that way only a rich white man could.

"On the other hand, you give us the reward for Gillian's safe return, along with the promise she can visit Miz Martha once a week, we'll consider the deal done," I finished as if he hadn't said a damn thing.

"You think you can blackmail me—" Kent blurted at the same time Callista said, "It's a deal."

"You can't be serious!" He yelled at his wife.

"What do you think is going to happen if you don't cooperate?" she snapped. "Not to mention we are starting family counseling next week. Now, put the damn case on the table and open it to show our good faith."

Her response wasn't quite what I was expecting, but Kent was backed into a corner, and he knew it. He tucked his gun in his waistband, a dumb move if there ever was one, and did as his wife told him.

Charlee picked out a couple of random stacks of bundled bills from the briefcase and checked them. She looked up at me and nodded.

I strode to the granite breakfast counter and retrieved my leather notebook. Walking back over to Gillian, I pulled out a card and handed it to her.

"Here's our number. Let us know how the family counseling goes next week." I glared at Kent. "If we don't hear from you by Saturday, we'll come and check on you."

She glanced at the card before she looked up at me. "I don't even know your name."

"I'm Hodges." I pointed my thumb at my wife. "That's Charlee."

"Thanks, Hodges." Gillian tucked the card in the pocket of her jeans and held out her hand. I shook it.

"Yes, thank you, Mr. and Mrs. Hodges." Callista fished in her purse and held out her own business card. "Call me tomorrow and we'll arrange those visits with Miz Martha." She also shook our hands.

Mother and daughter opened the door and walked out of the condo. Kent glared at me as he followed them.

Charlee rose from the couch. "I'll make sure they get home okay." She stood on her tiptoes to give me a kiss before she grabbed her purse and left, pulling the door shut behind her.

Gillian may be snug in her own bed tonight, but mine and Charlee's evening was just beginning. It didn't take much to break into the parish and city computer systems while I waited for my wife to return. No wonder Marquis was pissed. Kent had royally screwed him over, and he did it all legally. But there was information I could bargain with, so I printed it off before I rose and stretched.

Since Charlee wasn't back yet, I knelt and retrieved my jacket from the bottom of the food service cart. It had surprisingly few wrinkles. I took it back to the utility room and ironed the really bad ones.

Charlee walked through the condo's front door as I came back into the living room. She closed the door and leaned against it. My wife fought not to let the tears fall. The only time she cried was when she was furious.

"He lied to us, didn't he?" She swallowed hard and clenched her fists. "He gave Gillian to the Cedanos."

"According to Raphael, yes."

"What's the plan?"

I straightened the cuffs of my dress shirt. "We're gong to have a little talk with Marquis."

"Tonight?" A malicious grin filled her face.

"Yep."

If Marquis really wanted to keep his house secret, he should have taken mine and Charlee's phones when he and his people took us there. One shadowy figure sat on the porch swing. We pulled up to the curb, and Charlee laid a hand on my arm.

"Keep your hands visible since this is an unannounced visit."

I nodded. Marquis was not a man to underestimate. Nor were any of his people. I'd seen Charlee in action, and she could be deadly in her own right.

We climbed out of our SUV. She carried the briefcase and I held my folder. We walked up to the front porch. Thanks to a sliver of light that escaped the blinds, the shadow figure turned out to be Beau.

"Where's the girl?" he drawled.

The girl. Not Gillian.

"Home with her parents where she belongs," Charlee said. "I'm here to deliver the reward money to Marquis as I agreed."

Beau rose from the swing and held out his hand. "Give it to me."

Charlee sighed. "You know that's not how this works."

He chuckled. "I really wondered how much you remembered. Come on in."

When we entered the living room, Marquis was perched on his recliner. This time though, a frail elderly woman sat in the rocking chair. She was wrapped in a couple of quilts despite the hot, humid night and the total lack of air conditioning in the tiny shotgun house.

"Charlee?" The woman's face lit up in a brilliant smile.

"Hello, Miz Martha." Charlee set the briefcase in front of Marquis, but otherwise, she ignored him. She stepped over to Miz Martha and gave her a hug.

Marquis sat up and lowered the footrest. He grabbed the briefcase and popped it open. "There's only a million in here."

"That was the LaFontaines' reward for any information leading to the recovery of their daughter Gillian," I said smoothly.

"You cheating me, girl?" he growled at Charlee.

She straightened and faced him, but she still clung to the other woman's hands. "Do you want me to tell Miz Martha everything?"

The old man's eyes narrowed. "Do you have any idea what he's about?"

"Yes, we do," I said. "We also know how he cheated you out of a federal grant to rebuild the ward."

"You've been digging in my business, boy?"

Violence whispered through the room, so I needed to talk fast. "You should have told Charlee and me the truth from the beginning. We would have helped you. Best we can do is even the tables against Kent LaFontaine. But you and I need to make a deal first."

"What kind of deal are you talking about?" But Marquis cocked his head, which meant he was listening.

"With everything going on in New Orleans, you don't need trouble with the Mateo Cartel, which is what will happen if the Cedanos get arrested because you double-crossed them." I held up my manila folder. "In return for the statue you were supposed to deliver to the brothers, I'll give you a way to beat Kent LaFontaine at his own game."

"And how do I know what you have there is worth the same as the statue?"

"Because Charlee loves you and Miz Martha," I said. "And since you questioned my integrity, you've got to name one of the elementary schools you build after your wife in addition to giving us the statue."

Marquis' eyebrows tried to climb off his wrinkly forehead. Behind me, Beau whistled. The old man nodded, and his lackey brushed past me to go deeper into the house.

When Beau returned, he carried a wooden box roughly two feet long, six inches wide, and six inches deep. He carefully handed the box to Charlee, who was forced to release Miz Martha in order to accept it.

"Sit, child." Miz Martha patted the ottoman next to her. "Take a look."

Charlee perched on the brown upholstered footstool and lifted the lid. Curious, I crossed to her and looked over her shoulder. The cylindrical object was wrapped in white cotton cloth. She carefully lifted the item and unrolled the fabric.

The white marble statue looked like it could step from my wife's grip. The stone woman's right hand reached up as if to pluck something from the air. Or maybe fruit from a marble tree. I wasn't the art expert Charlee was, but even I could acknowledge the mastery of the piece.

Charlee looked at Marquis. "Is this what I think it is?"

The old man nodded.

"Could you tell me?" I murmured.

"It's Eve before the Fall." Charlee carefully rewrapped the statue. "An unknown Rodin. The rumor, or urban legend, is he destroyed her after an accident destroyed another piece."

"That's the guy who did The Thinker, right?" I asked.

"Yes." Charlee caressed the cotton.

"Satisfied, girl?" Marquis said.

She nodded and replaced the lid on the box.

I crossed back to the old man and handed over the folder. "I noticed your shell company hadn't put any bids in on these projects."

Marquis opened the folder and leafed through the pages. He looked up at me. "These are supposed to be sealed bids."

I shrugged. "Well, the county or the city has to open

them in order to make a decision." I gestured at the folder. "You've got a three days to get your bids in, but if you only target LaFontaine's bids, someone's going to get suspicious."

He laughed. "I see why Charlee keeps you around."

"Does this mean we'll never see Gillian again?" Miz Martha's voice quavered.

"No, ma'am," I replied. "I'm supposed to talk to her mother in the morning about weekly visits. I think she wants to meet you, too, if you don't mind."

"Course not." Miz Martha giggled. "How long are you in town, Charlee?"

"Long enough for a couple of visits." My wife smiled. "But it's late. You need your rest if you're spending the week socializing, and I need some sleep if I'm going to keep up with you."

Charlee stood up and handed me the box before she leaned over and kissed Miz Martha on the cheek. "I'll call you in the morning."

We left the house and climbed into our SUV. That went smoother than I thought it would. Underneath his gangster persona, Marquis was a businessman at heart.

"Do we have to give this to the Cedanos?" Charlee whined. "All this beauty will never be seen by the public."

"Is that the real reason you put the Mona Lisa back?" I glanced at her as I drove. "You would deprive all those school children if you kept it?"

She laughed. "Actually, it was a bet with Montague

I couldn't get in and out of the Louvre three nights in a row."

"I'm not asking what you kept from there."

"Are we done after the last stop?" She had to bring up our final meeting.

"Let me guess." I grinned. "You need some beignets."

"Damn right."

<hr>

We arrived back at the condo building in the CBD. First, I collected the food service cart. As I suspected when we reached the sixth floor, Lauren Biggs's birthday shindig was still going full blast. Luckily the catering manager had already left, but the kid who helped me clean out the cart checked the equipment.

"Don't worry." He grinned. "I can buff the scratches."

I gave him a couple more bills just for offering to cover for me.

Charlee waited for me by Unit 615. At my nod, she knocked.

This time, Gabriel answered the door. "Hey, gorgeous!" His flirty smile disappeared when he spotted me. "Who are you?"

Charlee looked at the box in her arms and then at Gabriel again. "We're fixers for certain parties who don't wish to see the Mateo Cartel and the Marquis Crewe start a war over a gift your boss wants for his daughter's wedding."

He blinked before he stepped out of the way. "We'll listen."

We entered their condo. Raphael lay on the couch, one pack of frozen peas over his eyes and nose and another pack on his crotch. He lifted the upper bag of peas, caught sight of me, and yelled, "Oh, hell no! Where's my gun?"

"Sorry about before, man." I held up both hands with my fingers spread. "The point had to be made."

Raphael forced himself into a sitting position. "That's him. The one who took the kid."

Gabriel eyed me and shook his head. "That's the gringo who busted you up?"

"Do you have someone who can authenticate the piece?" Charlee interjected.

"My brother." Gabriel inclined his head. Charlee handed him the box.

"Really?" I said.

"You got a problem, *ese*?" Raphael sneered.

"Gentlemen, can we please stick to business?" Gabriel rolled his eyes. "I'd like to get this over with and go home."

He took the box over to Raphael, who reverently sat the box on the coffee table. Raphael went through the same procedure Charlee did an hour before, unwrapping and checking the statue thoroughly, though he deigned to touch the marble. He finally nodded. Gabriel released the breath he didn't realize he was holding.

"It's been pleasure, gentlemen." Charlee bobbed her head and headed for the door.

"Hey, *ese*," Raphael said. His eyes could have killed me if they were steel knives. "We ever cross paths again, you'll be on the receiving end."

"And here I was going to ask if you wanted some beignets," I said. "We're headed to Café Du Monde."

"I think we'll pass this time." Gabriel grinned. "But thanks."

A half hour after we cleaned up the condo we borrowed, Charlee and I sat at a table, sipping café au lait and getting powdered sugar all over the place as we ate our beignets.

"You okay, baby?" I asked.

She brushed at the white specks on her party dress. "Yeah, I knew what Marquis was. I've always known. I let my sentimentality for Miz Martha get in the way."

"Look if you don't want to stay here for another couple of weeks—"

"How long?"

"What?" I knew what she was asking, but part of me wanted to save her from the pain.

"I know you, baby." She curled her sticky fingers around mine. "You would have hacked Miz Martha's medical records to make sure Marquis wasn't playing me from that angle. How long does she have?"

I had to turn away from her. The pain of when Grams died still clung to me. She'd been the one foster parent who gave a shit about any of us. I'd do just about anything to save Charlee from that ache.

"Baby?" She squeezed my fingers.

"Maybe two months," I admitted.

"Then we need to stay." She nodded as if answering a question deep inside herself.

"Whatever you need, baby." I pulled her close and kissed her forehead. "Whatever you need."

About the Author

SUZAN HARDEN transitioned from writing information technology manuals for companies and legal articles for a law enforcement magazine to her first love, fantasy and science fiction in all their forms. She's the author of the Bloodlines, the 888-555-HERO, and the Justice series.

Turn the Page
for a Special Bonus

Excerpts from Suzan Harden's

popular series:

Bloodlines

Justice

888-555-HERO

Blood Magick

Chapter 1

The bang of the auctioneer's gavel sealed the fate of Grandma Petrov's wardrobe. "Sold! To Bidder 665!"

Another wave of grief overwhelmed Dr. Bebe Zachary, not so much at the loss of the furniture, but from missing Grandma. Why had she let things between them fester for so long? Why hadn't she answered Grandma's last letter? She wouldn't be in this mess if she'd simply swallowed her pride.

No great revelation answered her guilty conscience as the auction house staff scurried to roll the huge wardrobe out of the way for the next piece. Soft coughs and murmurs interrupted the stark silence of the exclusive facility, but the heavy burgundy drapes covering the walls muffled even those slight noises.

Swallowing hard, she glanced at the man two rows down who had outbid her. Striking, with olive skin and dark, wavy hair trimmed in a conservative style, he gave her a mock salute. The glint of an overly sharp canine in his smug grin confirmed her suspicions regarding his aura.

Vampire.

Damn. One more problem she didn't need. How was she supposed to get Grandma's Book of Shadows now?

Apprehension sizzled across her nerves. She ignored him and turned her attention to the next item in the catalog, a milk can once used by Harry Houdini. Grandma's quirky obsession with Normal illusionists never ceased to amaze Bebe. Why bother when a witch had real power at her fingertips? But all the magick in the world hadn't changed Grandma's fate.

If only she'd learned of Grandma's death before the human probate judge had ordered Grandma's estate into receivership, an act for which she could thank her asinine cousins and their petty squabbling. Little did the judge know the real fight was over the coven leadership, not the estate assets. Ironically, the half-elven attorney appointed to oversee the estate knew exactly what he had been dumped into. He'd contacted this auction house, since it specialized in serving supernatural folk.

And supernaturals comprised the majority of bidders. The smattering of humans without abilities, aka "Normals," was most likely Family, scoping the estate for their supernatural relatives.

After another half hour, the auction of Grandma's possessions ended as quietly as it had begun. No other members of the Petrov clan had bothered to show. Probably a good thing since Bebe had the urge to turn every one of them into newts.

Grief mingled with anger and regret in her heart as she dodged the confused milling of the crowd after the auction. A quick glance assured her no one watched her while she sidled next to the wardrobe. She could cast a blurring spell to cover her, but the receiver had boasted that the auction house carried the best spell-detection charms available. Jail time and losing her medical license on a possible fraud charge wasn't worth testing the power of said charms.

She eased the door open, and the silky grain of the wood triggered old memories. Years ago, it had been her favorite place to hide, especially after her parents' deaths. The pain had been too much for a child to bear. Now, Grandma was gone, and old wounds she thought long buried ached with fresh agony.

Anger flared again at both Grandma's stubbornness and her two cousins' greed and lust for power. She had been close to both of her cousins once. Damn their idiocy that had forced her to return to San Francisco. She didn't want to be here. She didn't care about the family fortune or about power within the coven. She wanted to be back in Africa. At least Doctors Without Borders didn't consider her a pawn in some stupid game.

She ran a hand along the one of the doors smoothed from generations of use and tugged it open. Someone had to retrieve the ancient tome secreted inside the wardrobe.

If Grandma's Book fell into the wrong hands, the results would be disastrous—for everyone, not just her family. She stooped to disable the spell that secured the secret compartment at the bottom of the antique.

"What are you doing to my furniture?"

Bebe lost her balance at the unexpected tenor behind her and fell on her butt. Following the gray pinstripe-encased legs upwards, she met the eyes of her bidding foe. Pressure caressed her shields and receded. The weasel had been trying to read her mind the entire auction.

She climbed to her feet, her movements awkward in the straight navy skirt. "If there's something you want to know, then ask me," she snapped.

One of his raven eyebrows rose in amusement. "I believe I did."

She took a deep, nerve-calming breath. "I was examining the piece."

"And why would a White Rose witch be so interested in the interior of her high priestess's wardrobe?"

Oh shit, he knows! I should just go back to the hotel and wash the day away with a bottle of Jack Daniels.

Instead, she shot back, "Why would a West Coast vampire care about a witch's furniture?"

He shrugged, the motion displaying powerful shoulders. His thumb stroked the onyx ankh set in the heavy gold on his left ring finger. "I liked the piece."

"So did I." Tears threatened. Thanks to her family, she

had nothing left to remember Grandma except for the photos in her scrapbook.

He sobered and studied her. Again the pressure of his mind against her shields. A tiny thread of triumph ran through her. It would take a master vampire to shatter her protections. Her secret was safe.

He nodded at the wood behind her. "I'll let you buy the wardrobe."

Shock and mistrust ran along her frayed nerves, seasoned with a healthy dose of fear. Bargaining with a vampire was a dangerous proposition. Since her cousins and the coven elders admitted they didn't have Grandma's Book of Shadows, it must still be in the secret compartment. Bebe didn't dare let anyone get his hands on it, including this guy. Of course, his offer to negotiate could be a ruse.

She suppressed a shiver. "And your price?"

"Dinner with me."

She shook her head. Dangerous proposition was an understatement. She could be dinner for him for all she knew, though he didn't come across as a rogue. If he'd been anything but a vampire, she'd be tempted to take him up on his offer. She couldn't remember the last time she'd been on a real date. "How about my last bid and a couple of cover spells for your coffin?" she countered.

He chuckled at her forced attitude, the timbre sending a shiver of awareness down her spine. The bastard couldn't seduce her if he couldn't get past her shields, and she wasn't about to do something so monumentally stupid as drop her mental barriers.

He pulled a gold case from his coat pocket, withdrew a business card and held it out to her. She matched his unblinking gaze, her arms firmly at her sides. No power on earth could make her take that damn bit of cardboard.

One heartbeat passed. Then another.

Why wouldn't he leave so she could retrieve the Book? All she needed was a few seconds.

With a faint quirk of his full lips, he slid the card into the vee formed by the buttons of her tailored blouse, brushing the crest of her breast with his fingertips. His brazenness shocked any comeback right out of her head.

"If you change your mind, call me." He nodded and sauntered off into the crowd.

She turned back to the wardrobe, only to see the auction house staff cart it into the back in preparation for shipping. There was no way to access the compartment now, not without a lot of questions. Frustration at her lost opportunity welled up inside her.

She pulled the vampire's card out of her shirt with the intention of ripping it to shreds. Horror engulfed her at the name engraved in raised black ink. Caesar Augustine. Not any vampire, but the freakin' master of the western half of the U.S.

She squeezed her eyes shut. Both she and the rest of the witches were royally screwed.

A Question of Balance

Prologue

Two thousand years ago, every kingdom and tribe had their own names for the gods. These kingdoms and tribes battled over their gods, not realizing the different names were a construct of the inadequacies of human languages, when in fact, they spoke of the same entities.

She Whose Task Is Balance knew both past and future. She realized the danger such differences brought. Mortals destroyed each other, weakening not just themselves but the gods as well, because without their united worship, the gods withered. And far greater dangers lay beyond the world of gods and men.

She called Her priests and priestesses to Her on the shores of the Middle Sea. She bade them to sit at a round stone table. These servants of Balance were sorely afraid, for as She circled the table, Her form changed to that of each of Her Names, but always holding Her scales. When She reached the one empty chair, She was dressed in black robes, Her face hidden in a deep cowl. She drew a silver sword from nothingness and thrust it into the table. She then hung Her scales from the pommel of the quivering steel.

When She spoke, those who gathered trembled. And when She warned they had a thousand years to prepare for an invasion by beings from outside of reality, they shook violently. But they listened and spread Her Word.

The priesthoods of the other gods listened and prepared, for even their own deities attended when Balance deigned to speak. The rulers and people of the kingdoms and tribes listened and prepared. Knowledge was shared, and as a result all the lands grew and were prosperous. So wealthy the lands became over that thousand years, many, including those sworn to Balance, began to doubt Her Word.

Then the demons came.

Darkness fell across the world. First came the seduction of the demon's power, then the blood of mortals drenched the soil. Men and women pled with Balance to take pity on their plight. Seeing Her scales so weighted against them, She and her Sisters and Brothers took the field in all Their Glory.

It took another thousand years, but together, gods and men drove the demons back to their own dark realm. Or so men thought.

Balance warned them to be ever vigilant, but once again, mortals forgot because their lives are so short compared to the gods.

And the demons waited . . .

- The Fifth Book of Balance, Verses I thru X

Chapter 1

Since it was Rest Day, I was still in my bedclothes and breaking my fast when Duke Marco's messenger arrived. Setting aside the rich cinnamon bread, I glared at both the nervous young man and my personal assistant Sivan. "Tell me, is there a chance His Grace, his lady wife or his retainers might let me finish one morning meal in peace?"

"When the stars fall from the skies, Justice?" Humor edged Sivan's response.

My displeasure settled on the messenger. His bright scarlet face and hands quivered.

I smiled sweetly, but the boy wasn't comforted by my demeanor. My appearance discomfited nearly everyone the first time they saw me, my lover being the sole exception. "What is so important that your master could not wait for a reasonable time, like *after* Second Morning?"

"My apologies, L-Lady Justice. Duke Marco respectfully requests your presence. A-a body was found in one of the keep's wine barrels." His voice cracked on the last syllable.

Orrin was the third largest city in Issura and had the second largest seaport. While crime wasn't rampant, the city's main problem was disorderly conduct from sailors on shore leave. Or it was until I was assigned as the resident justice last summer. Even then, I was rarely called to investigate normal offenses like theft or smuggling, which the Orrin magistrate and his peacekeepers handled quite ably. It was for inconvenient things like this.

I shoved my plate away, wiped my mouth with my napkin and stood. "Thank you so very much for destroying my appetite."

The boy whimpered. From his voice and his manner, he was the highest ranking page available. No matter if he had heard the rumors many times over, my red eyes had made more than a few grown men wet their smallclothes.

"Run across the street, and request a priest from Light to accompany me."

"Y-yes, ma'am." He fled as if I'd summon demons to eat his scrawny hide.

Sivan didn't bother to hide her laughter any longer.

"You did that on purpose," I accused. According to the gossip I overheard on my way to the temple kitchen one evening, my nickname was the Red Justice. So far, no one had the effrontery to call me that to my face.

Sivan folded her hands primly in front of her. "He said he was instructed to only deliver the message to you, m'lady. Far be it for me to interfere with his duty."

I stalked over to the wardrobe in the corner of my private chamber. Inside were several sets of formal cloaks. To any one else, they looked identical, the black of the

Temple of Balance from hood to ankle. But for me, I could still see the blood stains on all of them.

Various laundresses' best efforts not withstanding.

Out of some sense of perversity, I chose the set that still carried the stains of the sorcerer Samael, a distant member of the royal family whom I'd illegally executed to save Duke Marco.

And the world.

Once I'd donned leggings, boots and a silk undershirt, I tied on my robes, pulled up the hood, and added my sword to the ensemble. In the half year since Marco's parents had been found guilty of treason due to their conspiracy with Samael DiRoy, little incidents had been occurring. Small challenges to the duke's authority. Carefully crafted insults.

It didn't help that he'd married a commoner who'd been conceived during the Spring Rituals, though the Lady Katarina was a healer of no mean skill.

So far, the young man had been holding his own. But a body found on his estate would only escalate the problems with the nobility, even if the young lord and his retinue were innocent. Nothing like a good scandal to stir the masses.

I reached the stables to find High Brother Luc, chief priest of Orrin's Temple of Light, already mounted, waiting for me with two of his wardens. Cold raindrops trickled dark purple tracks down his cloak.

I had to hide my delight that he came. "Brother, please

don't bother on such an ugly day. Either of your junior priests would do in this circumstance. Surely as the head of your temple, you have more important duties."

"Considering where the body was found, it seemed that our best truthspeller should accompany you, Justice." Amusement flavored his tone. Now that we were both permanently assigned to Orrin, we went through this dance of words every time we met in public since we could not often meet privately without arousing suspicions.

By the Twelve, I missed sleeping with him.

I inclined my head. "Thank you for your assistance, Brother."

Little Bear, one of my own wardens, moved to assist me on my horse. I glared at him, my foul mood spilling over once again.

Luc muffled his laugh, and the warden had the grace to say sheepishly, "My apologies, Justice. I forgot."

Reining in my temper, I said, "I understand, but this behavior must stop."

"Before she knocks someone's teeth out," Luc added. Like Sivan earlier, he didn't bother hiding his laughter.

"Yes, m'lady." Little Bear bowed and turned to his own horse.

It was habit on the warden's part, I knew. Every priestess in my order was blind.

Every single one except me.

The wardens and clerks acted as the justice's eyes.

None of the staff at Orrin knew what to do with a sighted justice. Not that I saw the world as they saw it, but I had vision enough I wasn't helpless by any means.

I climbed on my precious Nassa and patted her neck. "Shall we discover what's troubling Duke DiMara today?"

Luc snorted. "I'd say it was his ruined wine."

I couldn't be angry with the page for spreading unnecessary gossip. Luc could charm the knowledge out of anyone without the need of a truthspell.

We guided our mounts through the postern gate, down the alley that separated my goddess's temple from that of Mother, and up Temple Street, the main thoroughfare of the city. The business district gave way to small shops and eateries. Orrin was rich enough that the streets were cobblestoned, but the winter rains kept most of the citizens indoors despite the absence of mud.

Small homes appeared between the merchant buildings. Gradually the shops disappeared, and the houses grew larger as we climbed the bluffs on the north side of the bay.

The DiMara estate overlooked the city and harbor, an imposing stone enclave that still bore signs of its original purpose as a fortress. A guardsman swung open the ornate wrought iron gate, a show of the family's wealth, as we approached. The duke's family controlled a majority of the Orrin harbor trade, and those ships they didn't own outright, they had invested in over the years.

Two stableboys took our horses while the guardsman

led us on foot to a warehouse on the left. The dry interior was welcome after our short, wet ride.

Orrin's magistrate, Malven DiCook, was not.

"'Bout time his lordship's pet priestess got here." He coughed and spat on the floor, close enough to me to be thoroughly disgusting but intentionally missing my boot. Duke Marco wasn't the only one dealing with insults and challenges to authority, but the ones aimed at me weren't so carefully crafted.

If I had the evidence Malven was involved in the former lord and lady's treason, I'd behead the bastard without blinking. But I didn't, which meant I had to tread lightly around the duly elected city magistrate.

And tolerate the sickly sweet odor of the damn licorice-scented dye he used to disguise the effects of age in his hair and beard.

He hooked his thumbs in his belt and rocked back on his heels. "His lordship wouldn't let me examine the body until you arrived."

I brushed back the hood of my cloak and stepped closer. Being a tall woman was handy at times. I met the magistrate's glare before he turned his attention toward the floor. Sometimes, my idiotic attempt to give myself sight came in handy for unnerving my antagonist.

He muttered the Cantish word for "freak."

"No," I answered in the same language. "I was chosen by the Goddess. If you have an issue with her selection, I'm sure the Reverend Mother could arrange an audience for you." I didn't add my personal opinion of his hygiene habits.

He jerked and shuffled a step backward. I didn't know whether it was due to my knowledge of Cantish or my not-so-subtle threat. Nor did I wish to probe his thoughts to find out. Mucking out Duke Marco's horse stalls would be a far more pleasant task.

Luc's amusement at the magistrate's reaction tickled my mind, but he said nothing.

"This way m'lady." The guardsman beckoned us to follow. He marched for the opening that yawned in the floor of the storage room.

Luc faced our wardens. "Two up. Two down with us." Without a word, one of his and Little Bear moved to positions where they could watch both the main door, the passage to the underground storage rooms, and each other's backs.

Marco's guardsman lit an oil lamp and led our retinue and the magistrate down the wide wooden ramp. The air was terribly dry for such a miserable, wet day. Small bowls sat in alcoves along the wall. The bone salt in them absorbed the moisture in the air to prevent mold and rot.

At the bottom of the ramp, my desiccated airways itched from both the mineral and the sawdust coating the floor. Despite the sweet scent of mountain pine, another sickly smell met me. The guardsman gestured to the wide double doorway to our right.

I strode past the guardsmen to find Duke Marco, his

wife and sister, his steward, and another household servant on one side. Facing them were three of the city's peacekeepers. A wine barrel stood upright between the two sets of observers. The tension in the wine room was more suffocating than the odor of death.

"You and your household seem rather intent on disturbing my morning meals, Your Grace." I nodded to the women. "Lady Katarina, Lady Alessa."

"Truly, I would prefer not to." Marco's grim humor matched mine. "However, the circumstances warranted your curious mind."

"Would it make you more comfortable if I provided you a knife to threaten someone with, Justice Anthea?" Lady Katarina offered with the same amusement as her husband. She rested a bright red hand over her prominent stomach.

Sometimes, the odd eyesight I'd given myself let me see things that others couldn't. Like the rise in the lady's body temperature. Knowing she was with child before she did had been entertaining.

An odd sort of friendship had sprung between Lady Katarina and myself over the last six months. Probably because we were both products of the Temple of Love's Spring Rituals. Definitely because I had saved her and her husband's lives from his deranged mother and the demons her pet sorcerer had summoned.

"That will be unnecessary, m'lady," I replied and brushed the pommel of my sword at my shoulder.

"I've learned to carry bigger weapons when you two are involved."

"If you're going to do nothing but joke with His Grace, maybe you should leave." The magistrate's irritation felt like steel scraped across slate.

I turned my gaze on DiCook. "I didn't realize you had been named the Reverend Mother of Balance."

"Your predecessor had a sense of decorum in these matters," he shot back.

Sometimes, I wondered if the elderly justice who held the temple seat here before me was willfully, as well as literally blind. But that wasn't fair. None of the priest or priestesses of the eleven other temples detected so much as a whiff of trouble with Marco's parents before it was too late.

Unless I'd totally misread their allegiances.

I had gotten lucky, and I knew it. Otherwise, we'd be neck-deep in another demon war now.

"Really, Sir Magistrate? In reviewing her records, I did not come across any accounts of bodies in wine barrels. Care to enlighten me?"

He muttered another obscenity under his breath, but otherwise remained silent.

The duke and his party wisely said nothing as well while I crossed to the source of the odor and peered inside. I couldn't distinguish much in the deep green mass because the body had cooled to the same temperature as the liquid it floated in, so I inhaled deeply.

I looked up at Luc who had joined me. "He or she didn't loose their bowels in there."

"She," he corrected. At my quizzical expression, he added, "Too much hair floating at the top of the barrel."

"Could be Pagonian." I shrugged. Both men and women of Issura's neighbor to the north only cut their locks during a period of family grieving.

Luc shook his head. "No. Hair's too pale even soaked in dark red wine."

I sighed. "I suppose I should examine the timeline before we pull whoever it is out of the barrel."

Luc grunted and looked over his shoulder. "Duke Marco, when was this barrel brought onto your estate?"

The nobleman's sister Alessa was the one who answered. "Three days ago, High Brother."

"Was the wine seal intact?" I asked.

The three nobles looked at the steward who turned to the man beside him who nervously shuffled his feet before he answered. "The wax weren't broken, m'lady, but the winery stamp weren't there neither." He shrugged. "We git 'em that way sometimes, usually in the summer. The top's melt."

"But this is the middle of winter," I said softly.

"During winter cleaning, the lads at the winery set the barrels outside in the sun," the steward volunteered. "The air temperature is cold enough to keep the wine fresh, but the direct light softens the wax."

"Sounds reasonable," Luc said.

Luc turned back to me. *We can always confirm with the priests at Vintner.* Out loud, he said, "With her being dead, I won't be able to track her."

I grinned at him. "Afraid the Wilding priests might show you up?"

DiCook stomped over to the barrel. "If you two are finished making light of someone's murder, maybe you'll get around to finding the culprit."

"Murder? Who said anything about murder?" I couldn't resist needling the magistrate.

His face turned a brilliant scarlet. "So this poor woman decided to take a swim in a barrel of his lordship's wine?"

"We cannot assume anything at this point." My Luc, ever the voice of reason. "What do you need, Anthea?" His question was for the benefit of everyone else in the room.

"Just some quiet," I murmured. I pulled off my gloves and settled cross-legged on the cold flagstone floor. With one hand on the barrel and one on a shard of decorative onyx embedded next to the slate, I concentrated.

The stone quivered beneath my palm, eager to tell its story. It paid more attention to the vagaries of the mobile beings than its slate brothers.

I tugged the strings of time with the stone's assistance, unwinding back to four days ago. Luc and the rest would see transparent figures moving faster than usual. I could only see gray ghosts drifting around and through the colored figures of the living in the storage room. Two phantom men rolled a barrel out of the room.

"Hold." Luc's baritone rumbled through the air.

I paused the release of the time thread.

"Names," he demanded.

"That's William and me," squeaked the retainer standing with the steward.

"Name," Luc snapped.

"Bartholomew, m'lord," the retainer squeaked again.

"I told them to bring up a barrel of the local rose for dinner the night before the delivery," the steward offered.

"Luc," I said through gritted teeth.

"My apologies. Continue." At least he actually sounded sorry, but I don't think he truly understood the strain of what I was doing.

I let the string of time the onyx showed me slide forward. Several ghostly men rolled barrels down the ramp.

"Who are the three with Bartholomew?" Luc asked.

"The man on the barrel with him is Julian, one of the Duke's retainers," the steward answered. "The other two are the vineyard's transporters."

"Do you know them?"

The steward shook his head. "Rubio and his son normally bring the Orrin shipments. These two said Rubio had hurt his back, and they'd been hired to deliver the barrels."

"Names," Luc snapped again.

"Th-they didn't give their names." A green sheen of

sweat appeared at the steward's hairline. "Their paper-work had the vineyard's seal."

Luc folded his arms. "Where did the shipment come from?"

"The Pana Valley," Lady Alessa and the steward answered at the same time.

"Lord Aleister DiGrove's estate," the duke's sister added.

Luc's concern matched my own. If this turned out to be a power play within the nobility, things could turn very ugly very fast.

I let the rest of the timeline slide through my grip. But once the barrel in question was stored, it remained in place until Bartholomew and the man he named as William tapped it this morning.

"Well, that wasn't a damn bit helpful," Luc murmured.

I thanked the onyx before I shook the feeling back into my fingers and rose to my feet. "Let's drain the barrel and get her out."

"Shame about the wine." Luc stepped out of the way.

I could hear DiCook's teeth grind, but he kept silent.

The steward and Bartholomew set buckets under the tap to drain the ruined red while the guardsman went off to fetch an old blanket. Once a sufficient amount had been removed that we wouldn't flood the cellar if we accidentally tipped it, Luc and I peered in the barrel once more.

I pulled my gloves back on. "Ready?"

"We can do it if her ladyship can't."

I didn't have to look at DiCook to hear the sneer in his voice. "My thanks, Magistrate, but I can't have you or your men vomit on the body and contaminate it." I hooked my arm under one of the corpse's shoulders. "Ready"

Luc grabbed the other shoulder. Together, Luc and I lifted the deceased out of the barrel. She was heavier than she should have been, her skin having absorbed a great deal of wine. On the shores of the Peaceful Sea, one couldn't help seeing their share of drowning victims. We carefully settled the nude body on the blanket.

I brushed the soaked locks away from the face. A sharp gasp came from Lady Katarina. I looked at noblewoman. "You recognize her?"

She stepped closer. "The face is distorted but—" She gave a sharp nod. "Sister Gretchen from the Temple of Love. She was my playmate when we were children."

I could feel Luc watching me, which was understandable. For the six months since my assignment to Orrin, I'd managed to avoid the chief priestess of the Temple of Love, but I couldn't any longer.

With one of her people dead, I was going to have to face my mother.

Hero De Facto

Chapter 1

Harri Winters skimmed over the letter in her hand. "Give me a break. Professor Venom? Seriously?" She sighed and tossed the letter into her inbox. "Dammit, I thought he'd gone straight." And a half-assed attempt at a threat was the last thing she needed today.

"He's not dangerous?" Patty Ames, Harri's assistant, plopped into the chair in front of Harri's desk. "Is he a wannabe?"

"He's a wannabe wannabe." Harri shook her head. "He's not dangerous. He's just annoying."

"What's he want?" Patty settled back into her chair with a groan. "Sorry. My feet are killing me."

"If you need to go on maternity leave early—"
Patty shook her head. "Nah. It's just been a busy day." She rubbed her belly and smiled. "Not long now."

Harri smiled back. Patty was a good kid and a great assistant, but Harri dreaded six weeks with a temp. Too many cases, too little time, and by the point she got the temp trained, Patty would be back.

"So, what's the deal with this Professor Venom?" Patty said. Her blond curls bobbed in the direction of the inbox. "He says he's going to melt City Hall, and everybody will die—"

"Unless we give him a couple million dollars. Yeah, yeah. Don't start running yet." Harri spun her desk chair and dug into the file cabinet behind her. "Hang on a sec. I have a picture. You gotta see this guy. He's a total loser." She pulled out the "Professor Venom" folder and spun around to face Patty again.

"You usually show at least some grudging respect for supervillains." Patty leaned forward with a frown. "Is it because he addressed the letter to Harriet Winters?"

"Uh-uh," Harri said. "He doesn't have the ability to carry out his threats. And I don't respect the villains. I respect their assets. The forfeiture on Doctor Malevolent's evil lair gave us enough money to rebuild the Commerce Avenue light rail station and replace twenty smashed police cars. Try getting that kind of bank from a superhero. Cheap bastards." She opened the folder and handed it to Patty. "Professor Venom."

Patty looked at the mug shot and giggled. "Arthur . . . Doohickey? No wonder he calls himself Professor Venom. He's so skinny. And that nose is . . . unfortunate."

"Drallhickey." Harri rolled her eyes. "Lots of desire for elaborate mayhem, but more of a minor annoyance. Biggest thing he's managed to do is melt the paint off a couple of benches in Founder's Green. Which were scheduled for repainting anyway. He saved Dale's guys in public works from an afternoon of sanding and scraping. Dale wants the city to give him a vendor contract so he can buy Venom's acid formula."

Patty flipped through the pages. "I don't see his superhero nemesis in the file."

"He doesn't have one. That's how lame he is."

Patty laughed and handed back the folder. "Oh, that's sad."

"It's all kinds of sad." Harri spun on her chair and put the file back in its place. "Nobody takes him seriously. Poor shmuck. He doesn't have the skills to be a regular criminal, let alone the personality to be a supervillain. I'd hate to see this stupid stunt to screw up his probation." She mentally counted the months. "Or has he finished it?"

"You want me to call Judge Inunza's court and find out?"

"No, I've got his P.O.'s number." She stretched her arms over her head and yawned. "But first, I need some coffee, or I'll be useless this afternoon. I'm buying. You want some hot chocolate?"

"Ooh, yes. Thank you. With extra whipped cream." Patty pulled herself to her feet. "God, my O.B. says I've got another month to go, but I already feel like I'm carrying a toddler around in here."

"Hey, you wanted to experience motherhood," Harri said, and immediately regretted it. She wasn't sure Patty had wanted to experience motherhood. At least not yet. She was twenty-three and all alone. She had no family Harri knew of. When Harri had tried to convince Patty the sperm donor needed to step up—at least financially, Patty shook her head, her eyes shiny with tears, and said that he was gone, he wasn't coming back, and she didn't want to talk about it.

Harri yawned again and realized she needed more than coffee to stay awake. She decided to take a walk around the park first. She didn't have anything on her calendar for the afternoon. She'd planned to be in a deposition all day with Seismic Shift, beloved local hero and—in Harri's mind at least—menace to society. But his attorney called at the last minute, claiming Shift had an emergency and they'd have to reschedule.

Seismic Shift had the ability to create pinpoint earthquakes, but not pinpoint enough to keep from making a mess, Harri often grumbled to anyone willing to listen. The last one had taken out the Lake County Retirement Home in his effort to stop a couple of kids who'd ripped off a corner convenience store.

The guns they had turned out to be plastic replicas. And worse, one of the residents of the home had died. Shift was damn lucky the dead guy didn't have any relatives to file a civil suit.

Harri kicked off her pumps and fished her sneakers out from under her desk.

But her job was to give the displaced residents a new

home. Sure, Shift stopped the bad guys, but he also made a ton of money off endorsements and licensing deals and those ridiculous comic books. If he was so damn civic-minded, why did she have to fight him all the time to get him to pick up some of the tab for everything he broke?

She'd spent a solid week reviewing the thousands of pages of financial and tax documents Shift's attorney had dumped on her in response to her discovery request. With the deposition now put off for another week, she wondered if she should go back through the pile to see if she'd missed something.

She slipped her feet in her sneakers and yanked on the laces. Going through the boxes of documents again would be a waste of time. Federal law gave registered supers broad latitude to protect their secret identities. Without knowing who he really was, she couldn't get near most of his assets. He had to be making more money than he claimed, but she had no way to prove it. She liked the supervillains more because it was a lot easier to pry money out of them. The feds didn't care about maintaining villains' secret identities.

Harri couldn't figure out why people thought Seismic Shift was so damn wonderful. It's not like he was the Ghost Owl. Canyon Pointe's street criminals might not fear the police or the other superheroes, but they were terrified of the Ghost Owl.

Over the last twenty years, he bordered on urban

legend. Lots of sightings, lots of stories, but like Bigfoot, only a few blurry photos. In fact, the first thing she'd done when her job granted her access to the federal registry was check if he was in the database. But if he really existed, he was pure vigilante.

Shift was registered, but he was not only a complete phony, he was a media whore. Yeah, he technically had a super power, but the rest was all marketing. From his financial records, she learned the shock of thick blond hair that stuck out above his cowl was fake. Not to mention, he was starting to get a gut. Not quite the sleek, chiseled demigod his publicist made him out to be. He looked about fifteen years younger and twenty pounds lighter in his publicity photos.

Harri pulled her dark shoulder-length hair into a ponytail, checked her teeth for lettuce in the small mirror she kept in her handbag, and frowned at the gray hairs along her hairline—there was a new one every day it seemed.

Both her best friends Aisha and Jeremy had tried to set Harri up with the colorist Aisha used at Jeremy's salon. But she couldn't afford that kind of money, not on a city salary, and she wasn't about to take charity from either of them.

There were a few times when she envied Aisha's position at one of the top firms in the state, but Grandma Harri had drummed public service and standing up for the little guy into her head from the moment she could walk. Besides, she would have ended up like Aisha with all her money going to her ex in the divorce settlement.

With a sigh, Harri dropped the mirror into her bag and slung the strap across her body. The city's superhero infestation hadn't done a thing to deter the city's purse snatcher community. Hell, one of the assholes had nearly strangled her when he grabbed her bag in the grocery store parking lot last month.

"I'm going to do a lap or two around the Green before I go to Java Joe's," she called to Patty as she walked out of her office.

"Forward your phone," Patty called over her shoulder.

"Forwarding my phone." Harri pivoted, marched back into her office, and punched in Patty's extension on her desk set.

Once outside of City Hall, the bright spring sunshine lifted her mood a bit. The park contained its usual assortment of transients, drug addicts, and the mentally ill, but they generally left her alone. Harri was petite, but managed to convey a sense of height. Eddie used to describe her as five feet of rage topped by two inches of woman.

It wasn't rage. It was . . . Harri didn't know what it was. Righteous anger, maybe? She hated bullies. She hated injustice. And in her experience, superheroes were bullies with commercial endorsements. People needed something to believe in. Instead, they got merchandise to buy.

She passed the playground. Two women held their

babies while their older children played in the sandbox. It was exactly the domestic scene Eddie had described during their last fight. The one before he moved out and served her with the divorce papers.

Harri snorted and walked faster, annoyed at the thought of her ex. Stupid Eddie, with his new perky young wife and squalling baby and another kid on the way. He'd wanted a domestic family scene Harri had ultimately been unwilling to give him. She had nothing against babies in general, but did they have to be so stinky? And so loud?

Harri told herself that she simply wasn't cut out for motherhood. An essential mommy-ness had been left out of her character and she was being sensible by acknowledging it. But with Patty's baby on the way, part of her wondered if she'd missed out.

"Stupid hormones," she grumbled out loud.

Crazy Jim approached with a hopeful smile. "Miz Winters, how are you this fine day?"

Harri sighed. Crazy Jim was as sad as they came. When he stayed on his meds, he could function. Barely. That he had to do so living on a park bench, while schmucks like Seismic Shift lived like kings, broke her heart. Breathing through her mouth to reduce the smell, Harri said, "I'm fine, Jim. How are you?" She dug in her purse for some money. "When did you eat last?"

"Yesterday, Miz Winters. Yesterday."

"You could eat every day if you went to the shelter."

At least until they closed it. The stated plan was to relocate it, but Harri knew better. The mayor had plans for the shelter site in East Downtown, and somehow, a new shelter would never appear.

Everybody would be so bamboozled by the super show, they'd never notice the bait and switch. The mechanics of local government were dull enough without having to compete with a grandiose parade of idiots in their tight, colorful Lycra costumes, creating crisis after crisis. But no help for folks like Jim because he wasn't super enough.

"Can't," he muttered. "Too many crazy people there."

She couldn't argue that point and handed him a couple of bills. Enough for a fast food burger and a cup of coffee. From experience she knew if she gave any of the homeless more they'd forego the food and buy a six-pack instead. She wished she could do more, but what Jim really needed, she couldn't give him.

He thanked her and went on his way.

She stomped across the street into Java Joe's and bought drinks for Patty and herself. She stuck with plain black coffee because she couldn't walk past Crazy Jim and his lost companions with a concoction that cost her as much as the meal she'd bought him.

Back at City Hall, she gave Patty the hot chocolate with the extra whip cream her assistant requested and headed into her own office. Harri took a sip of her coffee and set the cup on her desk.

Before she had time to sit down or even take her bag off her shoulder, somebody out in the hallway screamed. She took two steps toward the door before an enormous wall of hot air pushed her backwards against her desk. Stunned, she saw a masked figure in black step into the doorway.

"I warned you," the person said in a gruff male voice. "Now, I'll take my revenge for you ignoring me." Something green dripped from a tube connected to his outfit. The substance hit the restored wood of the doorsill and sizzled.

"Excuse me?"

"You cannot escape the wrath of Professor Venom!" the figure said.

That's not Arthur Drallhickey. The man was much wider and several inches taller than the real Professor Venom. Not to mention, Arthur could barely meet the eye of his public defender, much less Judge Inunza, after he'd been picked up on the vandalism charge for the park benches.

She should be afraid. This was a wannabe who meant business.

More people screamed in the hallway and Harri became aware of an acrid smell. Smoke, but with a metallic, chemical undertone.

The man in black lifted his arm.

Harri threw herself over the top of her desk and crawled into the leg well. The kick plate and drawers weren't going to provide much protection, but the reconstituted fiberboard was better than nothing. Liquid splashed with a sizzle against her filing cabinet and the wall.

"You're done, bitch." More splashing. Noxious fumes and smoke rose.

Whoever that was, he meant business. But why the hell would any self-respecting supervillain want to claim he was the nerdy, harmless Professor Venom?

More hissing and the kickplate grew hot against her back.

Harri peered around the edge of her desk. Her attacker was gone, but from her vantage point near the floor, Harri could see the carpet in front of her bubbling before it burst into flames. A lake of chemical fire, too wide to jump, simmered between her and the office door. She heard something liquid drop onto the carpet with a hiss and turned to look. The wall beside her was foaming and steaming. Whatever her attacker had sprayed, it appeared to be eating the plaster.

The steaming foam spread to the ceiling and a moment later something dripped onto her shoulder. It crackled on the fabric of her blouse. Pain seared her skin, forcing back under her miniscule cover. The glass top, protecting the wood surface of the desk, would buy her a little time, but she had to get out of her office, and she wasn't getting out through the door.

That left the windows.

The Canyon Pointe City Hall had been carefully restored, in meticulous historic detail five years earlier, after the friction from Blue Racer's super speed had started a fire that gutted the interior of the building. Harri developed a national reputation among municipal attorneys as an expert in winning superhero compensation lawsuits thanks to that case.

As part of the restoration, the building's seventies-era sealed windows were replaced with historically-accurate oak double-hung sashes. Harri's office was on the fifth floor. High enough to be terrifying, but low enough she might survive a fall with horrible life-ruining injuries. She could crawl out on the narrow ledge. From there, maybe she could find an open window. She felt her stomach knot at the thought.

A drop of the stuff falling from the ceiling splashed against the edge of the desk and hit her hand with a sizzle. She yelped in pain and made her decision. Better a fall than being burnt to death. She scrambled out from under the desk, sprinted to the nearest window, and threw open the sash. Taking a deep breath, she pulled herself through the window as more drops of acid splashed on her legs and melted her pantyhose.

Of all the days to wear the damn things. At least, she still had her athletic shoes on.

A wave of vertigo hit, and Harri glanced back. More acid dripped on her desk, setting her paperwork on fire. Including the Professor Venom extortion letter in her in-box. She couldn't go back.

She clung to the frame a moment, fighting off the

dizziness. "Don't look down, Harri," she said out loud. "Don't you dare look down."

Instead Harri looked up. A helicopter hovered overhead, a cameraman hanging out the door. He saw her and waved.

She let go of the window frame long enough to flash her middle finger at him, then resumed her grip. "Gotta move, girl," she told herself as a gust of hot air blew outward from her burning, dissolving office. "Can't stay here."

Harri took a few more deep breaths, forced herself to let go of the window frame, and eased along the narrow ledge toward the next window, which opened into Patty's cubicle. Before she reached it, glass shattered, and hungry flames billowed through the opening at the extra oxygen.

Nauseated with fumes and fear, Harri scuttled backward. She was trying to turn around when the ledge broke away from the building. Harri didn't have time to scream before she was falling through the air.

Eyes shut, she felt something hard hit her.

This is it. Funny, I thought it would hurt more.

Except she was still moving, but now she was going sideways. She felt arms around her, and she opened her eyes.

A man was holding her. A man who was flying.

A super.

God, I hope I haven't sued him.

A bright neon yellow and green spandex mask covered

most of his face under a dark gray sweatshirt hood. She had time to register a rock hard chest and arms before he landed and set her gently on her feet on the grass of Founder's Green.

"Who else is in there?" he asked.

"My assistant," Harri said. "Blond, really pregnant."

He nodded and took off again. He flew, sleek as an arrow, into her open office window. A moment later, he soared out a window on the opposite side of the building with Patty in his arms. He dropped her off on the roof of police headquarters, across the street, and headed back into City Hall. Harri watched him rescue five more people.

"There you are, bitch," she heard a familiar voice behind her. "Not getting away this time."

A cord dropped around her throat, but she got her fingers underneath it before her attacker could tighten the garrote. But she didn't have the strength to push him off her.

Garish lemon and lime flew toward her in a blur. The garrote loosened, and she heard a cry behind her. She turned and saw—

No, it couldn't be. Crazy Jim sprawled on his back on top of the crushed roof and smashed windshield of a parked car. Blood was gushing from his nose, and he moaned. In the distance, sirens whined.

"We need to go," she heard the masked man say. Before she could answer, he'd scooped her up with one muscular arm and soared upwards. When they flew over police headquarters, she heard the people on the roof clapping and cheering.

I never got to drink my coffee. It was her last thought before she passed out.

www.ingramcontent.com/pod-product-compliance
Lightning Source LLC
Chambersburg PA
CBHW060555100726
47907CB00005B/1377